LUCY and DEE

THE SILK ROAD

LUCY and DEE

THE SILK ROAD

Kirsten Marion

COMMON DEER PRESS

Published by Common Deer Press Incorporated.

Published in 2022 by Common Deer Press
1745 Rockland Ave.
Victoria, BC
V8S 1W6

This book is a work of fiction. Names, characters, places, and incidents are
either the product of the author's imagination or are used fictitiously.

Library of Congress Cataloging-in-Publication Data
Kirsten Marion—First edition.
Lucy & Dee: The Silk Road / Kirsten Marion
ISBN 978-1-988761-64-4 (hardcover)
ISBN 978-1-988761-64-0 (paperback)
ISBN 978-1-988761-65-7 (e-book)

Cover Image and Interior Illustrations: Shannon O'Toole
Book Design: David Moratto

Printed in Canada

www.commondeerpress.com

For my parents

CHAPTER ONE

An explosion shattered the morning air, startling Lucy Banks so she made a mess of the big red X she was putting on the Yangtze River. She glared at it. The only wall space she had left for her map of China was above her headboard. The rest of the walls were thickly plastered with brightly colored maps liberally covered with red Xs and blue arrows marking the spots where Lucy planned to travel.

She capped her marker and jumped down from her bed to investigate. The open window was only a few steps away, and a moment later, leaning out precariously, she saw what had caused the commotion.

Pink smoke billowed from the windows atop the tower jutting up from the old mansion at the end of the street. Dee was experimenting again, and it looked like this one had "not gone according to plan," as he would say.

She wanted to make sure he was okay, even though he'd escaped any harm so far and she didn't expect this time to be any different, and to help him with the inevitable cleanup. But there were a few things she had to do before she could safely escape the house.

Lucy headed for her bedroom door. On the way, she kicked two T-shirts, a pair of shorts, and one sandal under the bed and pulled the duvet up over a messy sheet. She picked up three issues of *National Geographic* and tried to squeeze them into her bookcase alongside the previous five years of issues. Giving up, she put them on top, underneath her grandfather's globe. It was one of her most-prized possessions, with its countries all different colors that blurred together when

1

she gave it a twirl. She longed to visit every country—at least she could dream about the travel adventures she would have some day. Although, it was annoying that so many names and borders had changed since her grandfather was a young man.

She hummed a little tune to herself. Next year at school she would start taking a proper geography class.

Her glance around the room fell on the diorama of a strange and exotic country, the product of her vivid imagination. She had spent the spring building it on an old card table wedged into the corner between the foot of her bed and the wall. It was her pride and joy, but it did seem to collect dust and cat hair. She pulled one of the T-shirts out from under the bed. She used it to give the three-dimensional model a quick flick and called it dusting.

Lucy looked back at the room from the doorway and nodded to herself. Now she could say that she had tidied her room.

Clattering down the stairs, she hit the bottom step with a thump. To her right, the TV in the family room blared the football game.

"Where are you off to, pet?" her father called over the ruckus of a crowd gone wild over a goal.

Lucy crossed the hall. Her dad was in his customary Saturday afternoon position, slouching in his cracked leather armchair, his stockinged feet on the coffee table. His big toe poked out of a hole in his left sock and a large bowl of chips rested on his tummy. Lucy's cat, Peebles, nestled into what was left of his lap.

Lucy sighed as she looked around the shabby room. There wouldn't be any trips to new places any time soon.

"I'm off to see Dee, Dad." He clearly hadn't heard the explosion over the roar of the television so there was no point in mentioning it.

Lucy's mother came out of the kitchen. "You need to clean up your room before you go out."

Parents were so totally predictable. Lucy rolled her eyes and then, catching her mother's stern gaze, said, "I've already done it."

She had her hand on the doorknob and was almost out the front door when her mother said, "Stop right there, missy, the laundry needs to be hung on the line. The dryer is on the blink again."

Lucy huffed a heavy sigh. The dryer had been on the blink since, like, 2013. "Why?" she moaned. "That's such a drag. Didn't you hear that explosion? There was pink smoke, Mom."

"I did." Her mother's mouth set in a thin line. "I suppose that boy is up to his silly experiments again."

It drove Lucy crazy that her mother refused to call Dee by his name. He'd moved in with his aunt four years ago, and ever since, her mom had only ever called him "that boy." But Lucy didn't care what her mom thought. She and Dee had been best friends ever since the first day Dee was in her class. Lucy had flubbed a science experiment spectacularly and Dee stayed to help her clean up the mess so she wouldn't get a detention.

"I have to go and see if Dee needs some help." Lucy made sure she put some extra emphasis on Dee's name. "And find out what this latest excitement is all about."

"I'll give you plenty of excitement if you don't do as your mother asked right this minute," her father barked from the doorway of the family room.

"Yeah, yeah, I'm going." Lucy's shoulders slumped as she followed the jagged crack in the linoleum that snaked toward the dim corner of the kitchen where the washer and dryer lurked. The faint smell of mildew assailed her nostrils as she pried open the door to the washing machine.

"Ugh," she groaned, wrinkling her nose as she pulled out a wad of soggy clothes. Why couldn't her parents get their act together and get the dryer fixed? She loved them, at least she was pretty sure she did, but there were times, like right now, when she wished she'd drawn a better set of parents—one where at least one of them could hold down a job. She would do pretty much anything to live in a nice house where everything worked.

Resentment filled her chest as she pegged out the clothes as quickly as she could. Her parents never even tried to make things any better. They just sailed along, telling each other stories about how the next job would be the one to make them all rich. All the while their house quietly collapsed around them.

At least it wasn't a big load of washing today, and she soon had everything on the line and snapping in a fresh breeze. But doing laundry was hardly the adventure that she craved. She made her escape, grabbing a chocolate bar from her mother's not-so-secret stash at the back of a kitchen drawer, before she was given another dreary chore.

As she walked down the street peeling the wrapper off the chocolate, Lucy heard another blast, and this time, purple smoke billowed from the tower windows. "Oh man," she murmured, "What is it this time?" She finished the chocolate bar and broke into a sprint.

Gravel crunched under the soles of her sneakers as Lucy rushed up the circular driveway to the old mansion. She loved this house. She knew that Dee often had to go home to an empty house because his Aunt Delia was an emergency room physician, but Lucy didn't see that as necessarily a bad thing. She wished that sometimes she could do the same. It would be lovely to have a house to herself, especially a house like this. The flower beds were mounded with early summer flowers and lined with pretty stones. The smell of fresh earth rose around her. In the distance, coming from behind the mansion, she could hear a power mower.

She bounded up the three freshly painted steps to the porch and approached the double front doors of the mansion. They were bracketed with yellowing marble columns on either side supporting the roof above the wide veranda. A bird's nest perched on the ledge that ran above the front doors.

She had to use both hands to lift the brass door knocker in the shape of a lion's head. When she dropped it back against the wood, a boom sounded behind the door followed shortly by the click of high heels on a hard surface. The door slowly swung open to reveal a tall, slim woman wearing a slightly harassed expression. Her hair was swept up in a messy bun that released strands of hair around her face, and there was a smudge of what looked like cocoa powder on her left cheek. Warm baking smells wafted toward Lucy, and she inhaled appreciatively.

"Hi, Aunt Delia." Lucy loved Aunt Delia. Dee's aunt had never seemed the least bit fazed that Lucy lived in the most ramshackle house on the street.

Delia Ringrose smiled as she wiped her hands on the apron covering her black skirt and pretty blouse and pushed her wire-rimmed glasses up to the bridge of her nose. "Come on in, Lucy," she said as she swung the door wide. She opened her arms wide and Lucy stepped into the hug, delighting in the softness and warmth of the embrace, and the faint scent of Aunt Delia's delicate perfume.

"Dee's in his tower," said Aunt Delia as she released Lucy. "But I'm sure you've already figured that out. He's fine—I went and checked—but he's made another unholy mess."

"Well, I'm here to help." Lucy smiled as she scooted past the older woman. Lucy stepped into a broad foyer with dark wood paneling and a diamond pattern of white and black marble tiles on the floor. A sparkly chandelier swinging gently overhead scattered prisms of light across the walls and floor.

"I'm not sure what experiment 'has not gone according to plan' today, but can you go up and take it from here? I have something in the oven ..." Her voice trailed off and she looked anxiously back down the hall toward the kitchen. A faint smell of a cake scorching drifted toward them. "Hopefully, Dee's already started cleaning up," Aunt Delia said. "And there will be a piece of chocolate cake ready for you when you're done."

"Sure ... and great!" said Lucy. There was no such thing as too much chocolate. She paused, one hand on the banister. "Are we celebrating something?"

Aunt Delia nodded. "It's Litha, the summer solstice."

"What's so special about that?" Lucy wondered.

"According to my Irish grandmother, the summer solstice was one of the three Spirit Nights of the year," Aunt Delia said, "the other two being Beltane and Samhain. It's when the veil between the worlds appears exceptionally thin." She turned and rushed back down the hallway toward the kitchen. "It's also one of the eight Sabbats, according to the Pagans."

"Cool," said Lucy as she mounted the main staircase up to the first landing. She loved it when Aunt Delia, normally a no-nonsense doctor, got all mystical. Lucy thought the world needed more magic and mystery. She turned left, walked to the end of the hall and then up the spiral staircase that went to the tower room.

The spiral staircase was steep, and Lucy's knees began to shake from climbing. Soon she was outside a half-open door on the landing at the top of the tower. The first thing she saw was the lab bench covered in a complicated arrangement of glass containers and tubes and jars of all kinds of strange-looking ingredients. A burner, still lit, was surrounded by shards of broken beaker, and a thick wet paste dripped onto the floor. Beside the lab bench stood Dee. His back was to her and he stared out the window, his clenched fists digging into his hips.

CHAPTER TWO

She pushed the door fully open.

It creaked and Dee spun around, his white lab coat swinging open with a rattle. Curiously, the inside was lined with loops holding vials of chemical powders in jewel tones like yellow, crimson, blue, and white and some other substances in liquid form. Lucy always thought the coat was to protect against the same powders and liquids, but Dee assured her he knew what he was doing. Three small instruments and an omnipresent notebook poked out of the pockets on the outside of the coat. The black leather-bound notebook was identical to the ones he had already filled that were now lined up on the windowsill, each carefully dated.

Dee sighed with relief. "Hey, Lucy. Glad you're here."

"Another fine mess, Dee," she observed as she crossed the room to a small bureau and pulled a cleaning cloth and a pair of rubber gloves from the top drawer. She wrinkled her nose as she snapped on the gloves. The room smelled of rotten eggs. The open window would sort that out soon enough.

He nodded, and his clenched fists slowly unfurled.

"What is going on up here? Your aunt said you were working on an experiment, and I heard the bangs and saw the smoke."

Dee pushed his hand through his hair until it looked like a hedgehog sitting on his head. "I got some new equipment today." He gestured toward a lab bench. A copper pot sat on a gas ring. In it a thick yellow substance blurped. A tangle of glass tubing and copper rings captured the rising steam. Lucy joined him to watch the steam progress until it coalesced into a green liquid that dripped into a beaker.

"I'm working on a very important old alchemical experiment, the green lion. It promises to change lead into gold." He pointed to a pile of rocks. Some were a silvery blue while others were a dull gray. "So I tried it."

"Does alchemy actually work? I heard it was just what people practicing magic said they were doing, centuries ago, to avoid being tried for witchcraft."

"Alchemy was the way early scientists described their work. It showed the early development of the experimental method. There was certainly no magic in it," Dee said a little stiffly. "I don't know how many times I have to tell you there is no such thing as magic."

Lucy decided to move on. Dee could lecture on science and scientists until she was bored to sobs. "What made the smoke?" She fingered one of the cool lumps of stone.

"I'm using this"—he pointed to the green liquid—"to liquify the lead. From that, I could've extracted the gold. But something seems to have gone wrong." He looked out the window again before picking up a cloth and crouching to wipe up the spilled matter.

"No kidding." She began wiping up the splotches of Dee's failed experiment from the work surface.

"Who's this lady?" Lucy pointed to the statue of a head and shoulders at the end of Dee's lab bench.

Dee looked up, saw where she was pointing, and looked horrified. "That's no lady! That's Sir Isaac Newton! Really, Lucy. Don't you recognize him?" He stood up abruptly.

"Sure, I do." Lucy took a step back from the statue, giving it a sideways look as she did so. "It was the long hair that fooled me ..." Her voice trailed off. She knew that was a weak excuse—plenty of boys had long hair—but it was the best she could come up with to save face. "I know Sir Isaac was the scientist who invented gravity."

"Discovered gravity!"

"Okay, discovered gravity," Lucy repeated. "When an apple bopped him on the head."

Dee smacked his forehead. "That old apple thing again. That's a—what-do-you-call-it? When something is a figure of speech?" He snapped his fingers as if that would produce the word.

"A metaphor?" Lucy supplied helpfully.

"That's it! The apple falling on his head is a metaphor for being struck by inspiration. What are they teaching in schools these days?" He cast his eyes skyward.

"Enough that I knew the word 'metaphor' when you didn't," Lucy retorted. "So, what else was so fabulous about Newton?"

"He was only the greatest scientist, the greatest genius, who ever lived." Dee waved his hands around energetically.

"Fascinating," Lucy said.

Dee had what Lucy privately called his Hero of the Month, a scientist from history he'd focus all his attention on for a period of time. Lucy had been trying to steer him toward some influential women in science, like the alchemist Mary the Jewess or the chemist Alice August Ball, but so far she'd had no luck. Still, she lived in hope. Dee always moved on to a new hero and surely he would pick a woman eventually. Though it looked like Sir Isaac might last longer than his past obsessions. Lucy wondered where he'd found a bust."

"He founded modern science and revolutionized the world! I want to be just like him," Dee said.

"And we both know that I'm going to be a great explorer and world traveler, like Nellie Bly," Lucy replied. "That's where all the excitement is."

"Science rules," Dee insisted.

"You're such a nerd." Lucy flashed him a generous smile to take any sting out of her words.

"Yep, true fact," he grinned back. "Hey, do you want to hear a fun fact?" Without waiting for her response, he rushed on. "It was Dr. Seuss who made up the word 'nerd.'"

"Even more fascinating," said Lucy as she examined a series of items on a table.

"And," said Dee, a little louder, refusing to let the conversation move on, "Isaac Newton was working on a formula to turn lead into gold. He started with sophic mercury."

"What's that?" Lucy cocked an eyebrow.

"I'm not sure," Dee admitted. "His notes said to combine one-part fiery dragon, some doves of Diana, and at least seven eagles of mercury ... but I think those names have to be code words. They had some strange words for things in the seventeenth century."

Lucy nodded. "So you're not giving up on your search for your parents?"

"No." Dee frowned. "That's why I need gold. You know I need money to go and find them."

Lucy nodded. Dee had been waiting for his parents to return for as long as she had known him. Both archaeologists, they had left on an important dig when he was nine. According to Dee, they were super excited. He said they had stumbled across a new and amazing place that they couldn't wait to investigate.

"Have you found out where they went yet?"

Dee shook his head. "It's still all very hush hush, and the foundation they were working for doesn't seem to know—or want to tell. But I'm sure I could find them, if only I had the money." He stooped again to continue cleaning up the mess on the floor but not before Lucy saw his lower lip wobble. "I just wish they'd send me a postcard or something."

"I know you don't want to think about this, but could they have had an accident ... or something?" Lucy swiped at a few more blobs with her cloth. *Man, this stuff went everywhere.*

Dee turned on her fiercely. "Of course not, I'd know if they had."

Lucy took a step back before asking as gently as possible, "How, Dee? How would you know?"

"I'd know." He thumped his chest with his fist. "I'd feel it here."

Dee was steadfast in his belief his parents were still alive, and there was nothing to prove they weren't. Except this continued silence. But would she burst his bubble? No, she would stand by him in his quest to find them. Lucy decided to retreat to safer ground and eyed the rocks again. "So, how much gold will you be able to extract from this piece of lead?"

"Not much," Dee admitted in a muffled voice. "Just a few flakes, in fact. That's progress but it's not nearly enough. What I really need is to discover the formula to transmute all the lead into gold."

Lucy continued cleaning and examined some of the strange and interesting objects on the lab bench for damage from the splattered liquid. There were glass cucurbits—round containers Dee used to hold the substances he was distilling from one thing into another, and there were several beak-shaped alembics used to catch the condensation from the distillation process. But one device looked new and different. She didn't remember seeing it before.

"Hey!" Dee's head appeared over the other side of the lab bench again when Lucy picked up the triangular device and turned it over in her hands.

"Don't touch that. It's an old and delicate instrument!" Dee scrambled to his feet with his hand out to reclaim the device, but Lucy hastened to the window without acknowledging him.

The big oak tree sitting squarely in the middle of the forest glowed with an eerie light as if something illuminated it from within. Her heart lifted. Could this be part of the magical nature of the summer solstice? Aunt Delia thought it was a very special day, but Dee wouldn't think it was different from any other. He'd just laugh at her if she mentioned it, so instead all she said was "Look, over there."

She pointed into the forest behind the house. "Is that tree on fire?"

"We'd better check." Dee grabbed a small fire extinguisher from under his lab bench and ran toward the door. "Come on, then! It hasn't rained in weeks. The whole forest could go up in flames."

They took the stairs two at a time and bolted through the hallway, the kitchen, and finally the back door, which slammed behind them. Brambles caught at Lucy's legs as they ran through the underbrush. She almost ran into Dee's back when he stopped without warning. "That's no fire, Lucy. Look!" His voice cracked with excitement as he pointed to the middle branch of the tree.

On it perched a red bird, its head cocked as it gazed down at the children. Flames encased the creature but didn't seem to be burning either the bird or the tree.

"Wow, that's bigger than a wandering albatross," Dee breathed.

"That's all you get from a bird that's totally on fire but not on fire?" Lucy stood on tiptoe to examine it more closely. "This isn't another one of your experiments, is it Dee?" she craned her neck to look up into the golden eyes of the creature. They were the most intelligent she had ever seen in an animal.

Dee shook his head and, holding his finger to his lips, motioned to her to walk forward. They were only a few feet away when the bird spread its wings and swooped.

"Did you see that?" Dee turned to Lucy. The bird had disappeared into a rock under the tree. "I wonder where it went. And how ..."

They looked on all sides of the boulder, which stood as high as Lucy.

"Shh," Lucy said. "It sounds like music and it's coming from ... here." She put her ear to the rock. "Can you hear it?"

"Music." Dee agreed, his ear pressed to the rock. "Sounds like my woodwind class."

"Why would there be woodwinds playing inside a boulder?"

"There has to be someone behind this lump of rock." Dee leaned his shoulder against it. "Or something," he added cheerfully. He put his shoulder to the stone and started to push. "Come on, if you give it a good shove too, then maybe we can move it."

Lucy shoved until she thought her eyes were going to pop. Gasping, she finally stepped back and said, "It's no good, we can't budge it."

Dee, red-faced, nodded his agreement. "There must be a better way." He thought for a moment. "Do you want to hear another fun fact about Sir Isaac?"

Lucy wasn't sure that she did right now, but before she could voice her opinion, Dee continued.

"His second law of motion states that acceleration is produced when a force acts on a mass. The bigger the mass, the more force is needed. We don't have enough force ..."

"No kidding!" Lucy massaged her shoulder.

"Yet ..." continued Dee as he turned to Lucy. He had a gleam in his eye. "I'll be right back."

Lucy sat with her back to the boulder listening to the music within it while she waited. The sun was warm on her skin, and she was just thinking that this had turned into a pretty interesting day when she saw Dee racing back carrying a large and shiny container.

"Duck behind that tree." He put the container in front of the rock, joined Lucy behind the tree, and handed her a pair of goggles. "Here, put these on. Safety first."

She secured the elastic strap over her curls and settled the goggles on her nose as Dee pressed a small device in his hand. There was a violent flash of light, a boom, and shards of boulder whizzed by the two two of them.

"I've always wanted to do that." Dee wore a pleased smile. He tore off his goggles and stuffed them in the pocket of his lab coat. He held out his hand and Lucy handed him hers.

"Was that a pressure cooker?" Lucy said in amazement, watching the cloud of dust now hanging in the air.

"Used to be, yep," agreed Dee.

"Your aunt is going to be wild." Lucy surveyed the few remaining shiny shards.

A shadow crossed Dee's face. "Well, yes. There's that," he agreed and then he stopped, his mouth hanging slightly open.

The dust cleared, revealing the mouth of a cave.

CHAPTER THREE

Dee's excitement over the pressure cooker explosion faded as he peered at the entrance of the cave. He was sure he could see more cracks spreading outward from the opening. It didn't look safe at all.

"Oh, wow! Let's check it out!" Lucy ran toward the mouth of the cave. "Come on!" She motioned to Dee, who hung back still clutching the tree.

He shook his head. "It's dark and there are probably spiders. Besides, we don't know if the blast created any more damage. We shouldn't go in until we can be sure there won't be a cave-in."

Lucy poked the edges of the opening with her forefinger. "Seems sturdy enough to me. Let's go ... just a little way. Come on, what could go wrong?" Lucy ran back, grabbed his hand, and pulled him toward the cave.

Plenty could go wrong. A rock fall for starters, Dee thought. Lucy was enthusiastic and brave but also impulsive. She'd gotten into scrapes because of it before.

There was a little rodent-like squeak and a scampering of feet as they entered the cave. Dee shuddered and stepped back, but Lucy strode deeper into the grotto. "It's bigger than it looks on the outside and it ends at the back with a ledge," she reported back a minute later. "Oh, come on." She gave him a sly look out of the corner of her eye. "Trust me. Who knows? This might turn out to be an abandoned gold mine! That would solve all our problems. You could find your parents and I could see the world!"

"I suppose it wouldn't hurt to take a look," Dee murmured, intrigued despite his initial doubts.

He shuffled onto the ledge and peered over the edge. Stone steps, covered with pebbles and, oddly, dried leaves, led down to a large tunnel.

"There seems to be some sort of light at the bottom. The tunnel must come out into the woods again on the other side. I want to know who is making the music." Lucy was soon in the mineral-smelling depths.

She cocked her head and called up. "The music sounds agitated and it's going further away."

Dee wrinkled his nose, sneezed, and came down the middle of the staircase, careful not to brush against the rough stones on either side.

He reached the bottom and paused. Lucy grabbed his sleeve and pulled him forward into the tunnel. A moment later, she stopped. "Oh wow!"

The tunnel opened into a cavern through which rippled a broad rainbow-colored road that lit the way. Lucy crouched to finger the material of the road.

"It's silk, Dee. Ha ha, it's the Silk Road! I've wanted to travel the Silk Road ever since I read about it in one of my *National Geographics*." Lucy's voice rose with excitement as she trotted along the glowing silk. "That one didn't look like this though."

"The Silk Road? What was that?" Dee prodded the shimmering fabric with his toe. How could a road be made of fabric and not be shredded to bits by traffic?

"The historic Silk Road was the great trade route connecting Europe with the Far East. And it traded new ideas as much as precious things. The travelers along that road changed the world! Come along." She slowed to a walk to let Dee catch up with her. "We're going to have an adventure, so the Silk Road is a great name for this one too!"

Dee wondered if any of the great scientific ideas had traveled the Silk Road.

They hadn't walked more than a few minutes when a long rumble and a crash came from behind them.

They looked at each other. Dee chewed his lip and Lucy gulped. After a moment's silence, Lucy cleared her throat and said, "If we are going to travel the Silk Road, I'll need my maps."

"We should tell Aunt Delia what we're doing, and I'll need my navigating devices," said Dee.

They turned to run back up the stairs and stopped. The glow had left the part of the road they had traveled, leaving the return journey in utter darkness.

"We haven't gone that far," Lucy said. "I'll see if I can find our way to the entrance and then come back and get you." Lucy plunged into the darkness. A few minutes later there was a yelp. "Ow!"

"What happened?" Dee shouted.

"I ran into a wall."

"There has to be a better way," Dee muttered. He stepped off the road and put his hand on the tunnel wall. Stepping cautiously into the darkness, he advanced toward Lucy. "If we hold on to the wall and keep the Silk Road on our right, we should come to the staircase in a few minutes. Wait for me. I'll put my hand on your shoulder and then we won't get separated."

"Good plan," Lucy agreed.

"Did you hear that?" Dee's voice wavered a few moments later as his fingers tightened convulsively on Lucy's shoulder. "Something scuttled in the dark." If only he could see.

"As long as it ran away from us, there's nothing to worry about," Lucy said cheerfully. A few moments later she said, "I've found the bottom step."

"Why is it still so dark?" Dee complained, his heart pounding as he stumbled up the stairs.

There was a grunt as Lucy pushed against the fallen rock at the top of the staircase. A few minutes later, she said, "It's no use, it's completely blocked."

"'What could go wrong?' you said. 'Trust me,' you said." Dee shook his head and tried to ignore his rising anxiety. "Now what?"

With a shuffling noise, Lucy turned away from the fallen rock and Dee heard her take a deep steadying breath. She always said that was good for anxiety. He tried it too. The fear abated and curiosity rose in its place.

Dee yelped in protest as Lucy turned him around and prodded him back down the staircase until they stepped back onto the Silk Road, now brightly lit again. "If we can't go back, we must go forward." She shrugged her shoulders. "Come on. I'll kill the spiders for you."

Lucy had only taken two steps when the rock face beside her glowed. Then it shivered and rippled. A stone nose emerged followed by a hooked chin, beady eyes, and large bat-like ears. An enormous mouth opened displaying large stone teeth. The face was almost the height of the tunnel.

"Who goes there?"

Dee leaped back and pressed against the far wall. Then he jumped forward again with a strangled sound. Who knew what was going to come out of *that* wall? "How did you do that—come out of the rock like that?" *Nothing should be able to do that*, he thought. *How can the laws of science be different down here? We're only a short distance from my back yard.*

Bushy stone eyebrows formed and waggled above the eyes, now the deep blue of sapphires. The eyes swiveled to regard Lucy and Dee. "Why did you hurt me?"

"Hurt you?" Dee fought to press down rising panic. He couldn't think for the life of him how they could have hurt this monster.

The terrifying face grimaced in a menacing manner.

"Yesssssssssss," it hissed. "I am Lord Petram. I am lord of the rock in this tunnel and all the other tunnels and caves in this world. You destroyed living rock. That hurts!" His eyes pivoted, and his gaze fixed on Dee. "You!" A clawed hand emerged from the rock and a long finger jabbed Dee in the shoulder. Dee jumped back with a squeak like a startled puppy.

17

"I take a dim view of children attacking me."

"What?" Dee's mouth fell open as he massaged his shoulder with the other hand.

Lucy nudged him. "You blew up the boulder, remember?"

"Oh … ah … yes." Dee's shoulders slumped.

"And?" Lucy prodded him again.

Dee looked everywhere except at Lord Petram. "I'm very sorry," he finally said, staring hard at the Silk Road.

"What"—Lord Petram's voice sounded like wet cement now, low, and dangerous—"shall I do with you?"

Dee grabbed Lucy, his fingers digging into the flesh of her upper arm. She flinched and tried to pull away.

He hesitated. "One moment." Still grasping Lucy by her upper arm, he pulled her aside.

"Let go of my arm. That hurts," she protested. Lucy rubbed the spot where he'd grabbed her.

"Sorry about that," he said.

She glowered at him for a moment, then her expression cleared. "Go on," she said.

"Lucy," he hissed. "If this Lord Whatsit controls all the stone in this tunnel, maybe he can roll away the rocks blocking our entrance. Then we can go home."

"We've come all this way and you want to turn back? Don't you want an adventure?" Lucy looked at him in amazement.

"Wasn't Newton fascinated with the unknown and trying to discover its secrets?" She narrowed her eyes. "Don't you want to be a great scientist like him?"

Dee stared at his shoes as he scuffed them on the Silk Road. "Maybe. But let's face it. I'm not a great scientist yet. No, I want to go home." This place and Lord Petram were giving him the creeps. Best to get out of here—at least until they had time to figure things out a little more carefully.

"Please, sir," Dee looked at Lord Petram. "I really am very sorry about your boulder." A lump seemed to fill his throat. "Please open the entrance and let us go home," he added desperately. An idea popped into his head. "I could try to put the boulder back together again!"

Lucy looked at him with astonishment. "You what?"

"Why do you wish to go home?" rumbled Lord Petram.

"Because I'm in the middle of an important experiment," Dee whispered. "A very important experiment. If it works, I can search for my parents."

"Harumph," snorted Lord Petram. "A noble ambition but it doesn't excuse the thoughtless attack. You must prove to me why I should let you out."

"How do I do that?" Dee said.

"You must correctly answer one question." Lord Petram's thick brows drew together.

"What if he doesn't get the right answer?" Lucy butted in.

"Why then, you will be staying here. Or following the tunnel to see where it goes." The walls rippled as though somewhere behind them Lord Petram had shrugged a set of massive shoulders.

Dee was thoroughly alarmed now, and his stomach roiled. "Okay, I'll try to answer the question."

"What is the quest of the alchemists?"

Thank goodness, Dee thought. *An easy one. I've got this.*

"They sought the Philosopher's Stone, the key to transmuting lead into gold," Dee answered promptly. His shoulders went back, and his stomach unclenched.

A grinding roar came from behind them, and a few chinks of light bled into the tunnel. Lord Petram had moved the blockage.

Dee turned to make his escape.

"Wait! Why did you blow up my boulder?" said Lord Petram.

Dee stopped and was about to respond, but Lucy beat him to it.

"We thought there was a fire in the woods, so we went to check it out. But it wasn't a fire at all," Lucy explained. "It was this amazing bird, all red and gold. It looked like it was in flames, but it wasn't. And we heard music coming from behind the boulder. We just wanted to see what it was ..." Her voice trailed off.

Lord Petram's eyebrows shot up and his eyes changed from

sapphire to emerald to ruby and back to sapphire. He hissed, "What are your names?"

Lucy and Dee took two steps back before answering.

A loud rumble came from Lord Petram's thick stone lips. "It is you. You are the children we have been waiting for. There is an important mission ..."

"Well, aren't we lucky," Dee said, moving to stand by Lucy's side.

"Indeed, you are," Lord Petram's mouth cracked into the semblance of a smile. "You can go back if you choose, but you may wish to go forward."

"Why would we do that?" Dee's eyes widened.

"Dee." Lucy pulled on his sleeve. "Lord Petram controls *all* the rock."

"Yes, he said that," muttered Dee, edging back toward the entrance.

"*Controls* it, you dummy." She gave him a meaningful look. "If we agree to complete this task, then perhaps Lord Petram will grant you something. It might help you to find your parents! Your experiments all involve rocks!"

"Oh," Dee said slowly. "Right." He nodded. "Well sir, if we choose to go forward, what will you grant us?"

"If you go forward and complete this task, I will give you the key to transmutation."

"Oh wow! Really?" Dee was stunned.

Rock ground on rock as Lord Petram nodded.

"Okay!" Dee nodded in relief. "Let's go!" Then he stopped. "Wait, don't you think we should know what this job is first? And just how dangerous is it?" he asked.

"Sensible lad," agreed Lord Petram. He sighed and the ground shook. "We believe the emperor is in grave danger, but the source of the danger is unclear."

Dee thought about that for a moment. "What emperor?" Dee's brow furrowed. He knew they didn't have an emperor at home.

"The Emperor of Sericea." Lord Petram replied.

Lucy's eyes gleamed. "Sericea? Is that where this tunnel leads?"

When Lord Petram nodded, she turned to Dee. "A new country,

Dee. I've never heard of Sericea. This is turning out to be a real adventure."

"Attend, Lucy," Lord Petram said. "The matter at hand is that the Emperor of Sericea is too young to rule on his own, so the queen is regent until he comes of age. We believe he is in grave danger and might not survive to take the throne."

"What are we supposed to do about it?" Dee said. "We're just kids, after all. Shouldn't you be looking for adults?"

"The emperor is about your age," Lord Petram replied. "We believe it is young people his own age who can help him."

"Doesn't the emperor have friends of his own?" Lucy asked.

"No. He still has a few guards and servants handpicked by his father, but that could change at any moment."

Dee wondered why the emperor didn't have any friends. *Although it must be hard to be friends with an emperor*, he mused. *You'd never be equals.*

"So, are we supposed to rescue him or what?" Lucy demanded.

"Absolutely not," said Lord Petram, "It's not your job to rescue him or anybody else. It's up to him to rescue himself. What he needs now are friends of his own who can help him stay safe until he comes of age."

Before either Lucy or Dee could ask another question, Lord Petram added, "Will you go forward?"

Lucy looked at Dee. Her face glowed with the excitement of an adventure. But Dee wasn't so confident. A question tugged at the back of his mind but faded as his parents' faces shone in his memory. Dee longed to see his mother again, her green eyes—so like his— were always filled with laughter. And he would do almost anything to once more hear her stories about ancient people and how they lived. She could take a shard of pottery and imagine a whole family from it.

He saw his resemblance to his father every time he tried to control his shock of unruly red hair. His father was more interested in the engineering and technology of old civilizations. Dee would love to build something with his father again, like the trireme ship they made out of balsam wood with scraps of linen material for sails and teeny tiny oars when he was six. He still had it in his bedroom.

The key to transmutation could get his parents back, and he wanted that so badly that he was willing to give this strange quest a try.

"Yes, sir." Dee nodded.

"Most admirable! We will help you as best we can." With that there was a dull roar and Lord Petram receded back into the tunnel wall.

"Well, that's that then," Dee said with resignation.

"Oh, cheer up," said Lucy. "It's simple really, we find the emperor, help him stay alive until he's ready to take the throne, get the key for changing lead into gold, and then it's off to find your parents. What could go wrong?"

"Well for one thing, I noticed that this rock dude didn't say what the grave danger was." Dee grumbled.

"Maybe he didn't know. Maybe part of our mission is to find out what it is." Lucy offered.

"And who is this 'we' Lord Petram kept referring to? Or was that just the royal 'we'?" There were too many unanswered questions for Dee's comfort.

The road of rainbow silk vibrated slightly under their feet and the light brightened.

"Where do you think the tunnel ends?" Dee said.

"No idea," Lucy said. "But obviously, our mission lies at the end. In Sericea." She savored the word and then said, "I hear the music again. It's beautiful. We have to find out what it is."

Dee stopped. "But how are we going to find our way home after without a navigating device?"

"How far can it be?" Lucy scoffed and promptly stumbled over a rock and fell. "Ow!"

Dee helped her up. "Did you hurt yourself?

"I don't think so. Just stabbed myself with this." Lucy pulled the triangular object out of the pocket of her shorts. "Uh-oh. I must have picked this up from your lab bench." She turned it over it in her hands.

"That's my octant! My uncle gave it to me. He was a great scientist. I told you not to touch my things!" Dee grabbed the device and then calmed down a bit. "In this case, it wasn't a bad thing that you took it. It will help us to navigate home using the stars."

"Not much use in a tunnel then, is it?" muttered Lucy before forging ahead into the unknown.

CHAPTER FOUR

Several hours passed with nothing but tunnel and glimmering silk.

"I wonder how long this is going to take," said Dee. "I wish I'd had time to tell Aunt Delia what we're doing. She's going to worry."

Lucy nodded. She supposed she should have at least written a note for her parents. "I'm going to be in awful trouble if I'm gone for too long."

"I wonder how time works here," Dee said. "We only have one chance out of three that we will get into trouble and two chances out of three that they will worry."

"How's that?" Lucy said.

"Well, time isn't as straightforward as you might think." Dee put his hands in the pockets of his lab coat and briefly stopped walking to rock back on his heels.

Lucy recognized the signs. Dee was going to lecture.

"We've seen that the laws of physics don't apply here the same way they do outside the tunnel. Lord Petram being Exhibit A."

Lucy nodded.

"So maybe time doesn't work the same way here either. There could be one of three situations. Option one is that it passes slower here, so when we do get back, maybe we come back a hundred years into the future like Rip Van Winkle. Our families would have worried about us the rest of their lives, but we wouldn't get into trouble.

Option two is that time passes faster here, so no matter how long it takes us to complete our mission, very little time would have passed at home. And option three is that it passes at the same rate. I like option two the best—they don't worry, and we don't get into trouble."

The road curved. Past the curve, the light brightened and the music grew closer accompanied by the sound of hoofbeats.

"What the ..." muttered Lucy.

Two creatures bounded out at them, and when Lucy raised her palm toward them, they stopped. They were the size and shape of enormous horses. Their scaled sides heaved with the exertion of running. One of the creatures stamped a delicate hoof, and its skin rippled along its length, the scales glowing like jewels.

Lucy fell momentarily silent. These were the most beautiful animals she had ever seen, but who knew if they were dangerous? She kept her upheld hand steady as if to warn them to keep their distance.

"Next time, simply knock." The first creature scowled. Above his furry face he had red antlers covered in silver stars.

"There is no need to blow doors up! You really upset Lord Petram." The other one's long eyelashes fluttered with agitation, and his blue antlers, which were sprinkled with gold stars, bobbed.

Lucy's head snapped from side to side as if she was watching a hard-hitting tennis volley.

Dee looked intently at the creatures. "Interesting. Is this a new species?" he murmured. He pulled his notebook from his pocket and fished around for his pencil.

"Who, or rather what, are you?" Lucy blurted out.

"We are the Xami," the creatures said in unison. Their voices sounded like oboes and their upward swooping beards waggled as they spoke.

"I am Ai," said the one with red antlers.

"And I am Zi." The other one extended a foreleg and bowed.

"We were coming for you," Ai chimed in. "We were so close to collecting you, but the explosion drove us back."

"You were? What do you want with us?" Lucy's voice was steady.

Dee flipped his notebook open and made his observations. "What's inexplicable now will surely become clear and logical when I think about it later," he muttered as he scribbled.

"You are Lucy and Dee, correct?" Zi fluted.

The children nodded.

"Then you are our assignment. We are here to carry you to your destination," Zi said. "Hop on and we'll be off."

"They must be part of the 'we' Lord Petram mentioned. They're here to give us some help. That's right, isn't it?" She turned to Ai.

Ai nodded.

Dee looked hesitant.

"And a good thing too. We have no idea how far we have to go. Do you want to walk the entire way?" she asked.

"When you put it like that ..." Dee shrugged in resignation, but a gleam had come into his eyes. "It will certainly be a new experience to ride a Xami."

"A single one of us is called a Xamu." Ai said. "Now do as he said and hop aboard."

Dee nodded and eyed the saddle suspiciously.

With some effort, Lucy scrambled onto Ai's gold-painted saddle, which was decorated with crimson designs.

"This is harder than it looks," Dee grumbled after his second attempt to mount Zi ended badly. His third time turned out to be the charm.

Lucy scarcely heard Ai's advice to hang on as he gathered himself beneath her and broke into a fast gallop down the Silk Road. Tears filled her eyes and spilled down her cheeks as, unbelievably, Ai increased his speed. Lucy could hear Zi galloping behind but could only assume that Dee was still on him. Surely the Xamu would stop and help him remount if he fell off.

The ride went on and on and on. Lucy's legs began to ache, and her bottom felt bruised when Ai slowed and finally stopped. "Hop on down, Lucy."

"We will take a break here," Zi said as he drew up alongside her with Dee, white-faced but upright on his back.

Lucy nodded and tried to dismount, but her fingers felt curled into claws around Ai's thick red ruff. "How much farther?"

"Quite far," said Zi.

"So, we will have some food and drink here," Ai chimed in.

Lucy looked around. "Here?" The tunnel walls were smooth around them and there were no signs of snacks anywhere.

"Here," Ai said and turned to the wall. Stamping his right hoof four times, he sang six rising notes.

With a grinding sound that raised the hair on the back of Lucy's neck, the craggy features of Lord Petram pushed through the rock. His previously sullen face brightened when he saw the Xami.

"I see you have found them," Lord Petram rumbled, swiveling his eyes to indicate Lucy and Dee.

"We never lost them," Zi objected.

Ai bowed over his right leg. "The children require sustenance, Lord Petram. Will you assist?"

"And what do you desire?" Lord Petram fixed his glittering gaze, emerald green now, on Lucy.

"We can ask for anything?" Lucy's eyebrows rose. She wondered how edible food could be produced from stone, but her stomach growled hopefully. She clutched it with embarrassment as heat rose to her face.

Ai turned to her. "Speak graciously to Lord Petram," he warned softly. "Remember, he controls all of the rock in this world."

Seeing Ai's frown, Lucy added hastily, "Your Lordship."

Lord Petram nodded.

"But how does that even work?" Dee wondered. "Where does it come from?" He looked around. "I can't see anything but rock and road."

"I can create anything you desire to eat. Now are you hungry or not?" Lord Petram sounded testy.

"Magic." Lucy breathed, her eyes shining. "I w-would like mac 'n' cheese with a side of f-fries," she stuttered.

"And you, young man?" Lord Petram's gaze softened to the golden-brown glow of tiger's eye as he regarded Dee.

Dee, his face greenish white, was looking hard at the ground and rubbing a sore spot on his backside.

Zi tapped a hoof and coughed.

Dee bit his lip, looked up, and sighed. "If you please, sir, I would like roast chicken with lemon potatoes and green beans with butter."

"Very well," said Lord Petram.

A grinding sound filled the air and Lucy clenched her teeth at the awful noise. A stone table pushed out of the rock and into the center of the Silk Road. Two large hands, their thick fingers ending in sharp nails, held out stone bowls full of lumps of rock streaked with glittering veins of different minerals. They were very pretty, of course, but completely inedible. Lucy's heart sank as her stomach gave another futile growl.

Lord Petram placed the bowls on the table before them. "Now you will eat."

Lucy began to protest, "But—"

"Many thanks, my lord," Zi interrupted. The Xamu closed his eyes in concentration and a warm breeze sprang up and flowed over the stone table. The mineral veins pulsed and glowed. Color suffused the lumps of rock, and they took on the hues of chicken, potatoes, buttered green beans, and mac 'n' cheese with fries nestled within the stone bowls, which were now a beautiful translucent green.

"Look at that, Dee," she whispered. "Lord Petram isn't the only one with the key to transmutation. The Xami have it too!"

"When you think about it," Dee mused, "all food is the transmutation of rock. It's a main part of soil, after all. Grains, fruit, and vegetables grow in the soil. And then, of course, animals eat the plants. If we have a steak on a plate, it came from ground-up rock. Lord Petram has just managed to speed up the process."

Dee ran a fingertip along the edge of one of the bowls. "Malachite," he breathed. He looked at the feast spread before him. "I wish I had time to study this properly."

Lord Petram grunted approval. "You have a good eye for stone, boy."

Hot food aromas filled the air as Zi turned to the children. "You may sit on our backs to eat."

The Xami folded their legs beneath them, and the children sat. Lucy regarded her large bowl of mac 'n' cheese. The cheese sauce glistened, and the fries looked crisp and lightly salted. She selected a fry and dropped it shaking her hand. "Hot!"

The smell of the pasta was making her stomach roar with hunger. She looked helplessly at her heaping bowl of pasta and then at Dee, who regarded his own dinner with some dismay. She turned to Lord Petram, who gazed down with a stony expression. "Could we have some cutlery?" Her voice squeaked at the end as Ai shifted beneath her in a meaningful manner. She cleared her throat. "Please, sir."

With a faint sigh, Lord Petram produced a fork for Lucy and a knife and fork for Dee. "Look at this," Dee said, holding up his glittering, white knife. "I think it's made from diamond."

"Really?" Lucy's voice rose with excitement. "That's amazing. And valuable, Dee." Her voice sank to a whisper. "If he's already giving you diamond forks, can you imagine what we'll get when we finish our task? We *have* to go on!" Then she switched back to a normal volume. "What's mine, then?" she said, handing Dee her pink crystal fork.

He turned it over in his hands and then hefted it. "Hm, I think this is corundum." He looked up at Lord Petram for verification.

"Well done, boy." His voice rang with approval. "Now eat, before it gets cold."

Lucy dug right in before noticing Dee prodding at his food. Turning pieces over and examining them closely.

"Why are you playing with your food?" Lucy's words were muffled by a large mouthful of pasta.

"Call me Mr. Suspicious," Dee murmured. "But this isn't natural."

He speared a green bean on his fork and, using his fingers, bent it in a curve. "It seems real enough."

"Hush, you'll hurt their feelings," Lucy said. "And wasn't it you who just said all food comes from rock?"

Dee muttered something inaudible and took a bite of his green bean.

The only sounds after that exchange were of their breathing and the clink of minerals against stone.

When they had finished their dinners, Ai turned to Lucy, his feathery eyebrows raised. "Sweets?"

"Oh, yes!" Lucy nodded with enthusiasm. "An ice cream sundae please, with extra fudge sauce."

Dee opted for a piece of German chocolate cake, and there were a few moments of silence as the children devoured their desserts.

Dee paused with his fork raised to his lips. "Aunt Delia was making the same cake when we ran out the back door and into this strange new world."

Lucy knew he was again feeling guilty that he hadn't told his aunt where he was going. "Think of the stories you'll have to tell her when we return," she said, trying to cheer him up.

Ai stirred under her, and Lucy stood to allow the Xamu to get to his feet.

"We hope you have been refreshed," Zi said.

"Now we continue ..." Ai said

"To our destination," Zi finished.

This time, Lucy found mounting the Xamu easier, but when she sat down, her bum felt like it was on fire. "Ow!" she cried.

"You will be a bit stiff," Ai said.

"Thank you, Captain Obvious," Dee muttered, grimacing as he settled into the saddle.

"It will pass," Zi assured them.

Once more the Xami broke into a swift gallop. The Silk Road blurred beneath them, and the walls of the tunnel appeared to turn to liquid. The air was colder now. Goosebumps sprang up on Lucy's arms, bare except for the short sleeves of her striped T-shirt. A sharp, damp smell stung her nostrils. She held out her hand and a drop of water fell into it. An uneasy suspicion rose within her.

"Where are we, Ai?"

"We are now under the ocean."

"What!" Lucy shrieked. Ai shied, and she almost fell off.

The Xamu recovered his footing and Lucy recovered her seat. "What did you yell like that for?" Ai sounded huffy.

"I-I-I was just shocked," Lucy said. She closed her eyes as the

Xamu galloped on. The dank air felt like it was being forced out of her lungs by a heavy weight and the increased pressure made her ears pop. All she could think of was the miles and miles of ocean pressing down on them. The tunnel walls swam before her eyes, and she thought she might faint.

She looked up at the roof of the tunnel, counting the damp spots as they raced by. Millions of tons of water were just waiting to crush them. She shivered as she hyperventilated. The reins slid from her slick palms as she pushed down a scream. Tilting dangerously far to the right, she nearly toppled over before Ai slowed to a halt.

Zi pulled up beside him.

"What is wrong?" Ai inquired; his tone was concerned.

"You okay?" Dee's forehead wrinkled as he turned to look at Lucy. "You don't look great."

"I-I don't like this. I can't breathe," Lucy choked out. "I'm afraid all the water above us will come crashing through the tunnel walls."

"Here's an interesting thing," Dee said. "The curvature of the tunnel walls means it's able to withstand much greater force than if they were straight."

"Don't be afraid," Ai reassured her. "Lord Petram holds these rocks fast. No harm will come to you. I can assure you of that. May we proceed now?"

Barely reassured, Lucy nodded.

The Xami rapidly resumed a gallop. On and on and on rode Lucy and Dee. What seemed like hours dragged by, and Lucy wondered if they would ever stop. Her head pounded with fatigue. She began to think this was a nightmare that would never end.

In her misery, Lucy almost didn't notice when the air freshened with a faint breeze, and she barely heard Ai call out, "Look!"

A glimmer of light flickered ahead. Gradually, it grew larger and larger until daylight poured in from the mouth of the tunnel. The children blinked and shielded their eyes as the two Xami sprang from the mouth of the tunnel into the dazzling sunlight. Her heart lifted as Ai said, "We've reached the land of Sericea."

CHAPTER FIVE

Dee glanced at Lucy. He quietly sighed with relief as he noted her look of excitement was back. She seemed to have weathered her ordeal in the tunnel and bounced right back.

A slight breeze lifted the end of Lucy's curls and dissipated the puffs of golden dust the Xami's hooves raised as they set off along the road. There were tall stands of bamboo overhanging the road and thick grasses bordered either side. Dee tapped Zi on the neck to get his attention.

"So this is Sericea?" He looked around. He felt the excitement of an explorer discovering a new continent. Who knew what the scientific opportunities were here? "It looks very different from home."

The bamboo rustled overhead casting flickering shadows on the winding dirt road that stretched before them.

"Yes," Zi confirmed. "It is an ancient land ruled by the emperor, who ensures unity of all under heaven."

"Sounds nice." Dee's mouth lifted in a half smile.

"It is," Zi's head bobbed in agreement. "When it works."

"Lord Petram told us we were going to Sericea. But why have I never heard about it before?" Lucy asked as she twisted on Ai's golden saddle to see all around.

"Because it likes to stay hidden," said Ai.

Dee's eyebrows shot up. "What do you mean, 'it likes to stay hidden'? How is that even possible?"

Zi replied, "Many places exist that choose to remain hidden from outsiders. But those who are meant to be there, will find their way to them. However, they require special access."

"Like a portal?" said Lucy

"Just so." Ai turned his head to look at her.

A burst of birdsong came from a towering clump of heavily scented flowers that resembled large, white trumpets.

"Can we get back through the tunnel?" said Dee. "When we're done, I mean."

"Probably." Zi gave an unconcerned movement of his shoulders. "It doesn't matter. You are needed here now." He stamped a forefoot for emphasis.

The question that had been hammering at the back of Dee's mind ever since Lord Petram had given them their mission finally popped out. "How long is it until the emperor comes of age?"

"You will have to ask him," Zi said vaguely.

"You don't know?" Dee was astonished. "If you don't have an exact date, can't you at least narrow it down?"

The Xamu shrugged. "Not long. When you've lived as long as we have, anything less than a decade is unimportant."

Dee wasn't sure about staying in Sericea with no definite return date or time. He chewed his lower lip as he weighed the fallout of worrying Aunt Delia against the prospect of finding his parents. Aunt Delia would understand, he assured himself. She wanted his parents to come home too, he was sure of it. And how long could it be? If the young emperor was about their age, it couldn't be too long.

Plus, he was strangely excited about this extraordinary new place. This was his chance to make some new scientific discoveries. There were clearly different laws of science here, but how different? Did the plants behave as differently as the rock? Were there more strange animal species? The possibilities stretched out before him, giving him a tingly sensation in the pit of his stomach. He thought he might be starting to understand the excitement his parents felt when they discovered their lost city.

He studied the back of Zi's long neck. The blue ruff was thick and soft, like the ruff on the big chow they had when he was little, and it ended somewhere under Dee's saddle. Shimmering scales, like a blue Malaysian coral snake's, covered his body. Dee looked down and saw Zi had shiny black hooves, like a horse. *But horses don't have sparkly antlers.*

Well—Dee sat back in the saddle—*I might as well start my scientific inquiries right here and right now.*

"Zi, I was wondering, what sort of species are you? You have the features of multiple animals. Are you a product of crossbreeding?"

Zi turned his head to fix Dee with a gaze out of one glowing eye. "We were made, yes. We have the fleetness of the white golden-horned antelope, the courage of the lion, the power of the dragon, and the stamina of the horse."

Dragons, Dee mentally noted. *I'll come back to that later.*

"Are there female Xami? Are you able to reproduce?"

"Dee! Personal question!" Lucy looked shocked.

He felt a flush creep up his neck. "Sorry, it's just that where we come from, mules, the product of crossbreeding between horses and donkey, are sterile."

"A Xamu can be either male or female. But we have to be individually made." Zi sighed. "Unfortunately, the learning for that was lost four centuries ago. No more of us have been made since. It's becoming a worry."

Centuries! Dee would have staggered if he hadn't been sitting in a saddle. "How old are you, Zi?"

Zi appeared to think for a moment. "About seven hundred. We live almost indefinitely unless something drastic befalls us."

"How many Xami are there?" Lucy wondered aloud.

"There are only six of us left where once there were hundreds."

"Something drastic?" Dee asked softly.

Zi nodded.

Dee fell silent, and there was only the sound of the Xami's hooves and the faint whirr of insect life.

Moments later, Lucy coughed and said, "I still don't quite understand why it's up to us to help the emperor stay safe until he comes of age. Why not someone from here? We're bound to make mistakes, dangerous mistakes, because we don't have a clue about the people or the places here. Why can't you and Lord Petram do something yourselves? You seem to be very powerful."

"We aren't human," Ai explained, "the Xami, Lord Petram. We don't think like humans. Our thought is seen in cool, serene colors, and it flows smoothly. Human thought is often reds and blacks, tangled in complicated knots, twisting in every direction. We can't comprehend how humans plan future actions."

"You can read minds?" Lucy inquired.

Ai shook his head. "We just see the colors and shapes and sense the state of the mind.

"So, you don't have any idea how bad the danger is or could get?" Dee said.

"Just so," said Ai. "It is all clouded around the young emperor. We cannot even see where the danger comes from, and that is not right."

"We need you two to tell us what is behind the clouds we're seeing. Adults can't get close to the emperor like you can," added Zi.

"If Lord Petram is lord of all rock," Dee wondered, "why can't he move through the palace to see what's going on? Surely some of it is made of stone."

"He can only move through living rock. Rock still in the earth," said Ai.

"I don't understand." Lucy frowned. "Living rock?"

"If I cut your leg off, child, could you still control it?" Zi turned his head to regard her.

"Short of picking it up and hitting someone with it, I suppose not," Lucy mused.

"Exactly. When rock is cut from the earth, Lord Petram is severed from it. Like this road, for instance. He can't communicate with us through it, but we could call him through that boulder over there. It is still wild."

The concept of wild rock is pretty wild itself, Dee thought as they trotted on.

Lucy, too, appeared lost in thought as they traveled on until the sun was just about to touch the horizon. Then the Xami veered off the Silk Road and into a clearing.

"We will stop here for the night and continue our journey tomorrow."

It had been a long and eventful day, and Dee was grateful to finally slide from Zi's back. They were in a large clearing, surrounded by stately trees with a smooth white bark. Clumps of bushes with thick green foliage and bright flowers the size and shape of a softball clustered under the trees.

"Do you need food?" Ai asked.

Dee nodded, he always needed food. He was a growing boy.

There were some small rocks and a pile of pebbles scattered around the edge of the clearing. Ai walked over to a rock, stamped his right hoof four times, and sang the same six rising notes used to call Lord Petram in the tunnel.

A miniature face of the Lord of Rock appeared. "Yes?" His voice wasn't diminished despite his smaller size. It boomed as loudly as in the tunnel.

"The children require sustenance, my lord." Ai said.

In short order, Lucy and Dee had plates of their favorite foods in their hands and they dug in with enthusiasm. The Xami cropped at the thick grasses in the clearing.

Dee was pleasantly drowsy now, but a question had been nagging at him. He opened his mouth to ask it when Lucy beat him to it.

"Where will we sleep?" Lucy looked around. "And how will we stay warm? It's getting colder and I've only got shorts and a T-shirt on."

Dee wasn't dressed very warmly either, but at least he had his lab coat.

Lord Petram focused his gaze on the pile of pebbles. As Dee watched, they seemed to waver, then elongate, smooth out, and stretch further and further, like the pie crust Aunt Delia used to make. When they formed a very large sheet, the sheet tore in two.

Lucy went and picked up a piece. It looked heavy in her hand but rippled like material. "It's a woolen blanket, Dee. And there's one for each of us."

36

"Wow!" Dee exclaimed. "This is all wrong." He waved a hand at the blankets. "This is not behaving according to the laws of physics."

"Maybe they aren't laws. Maybe they're just suggestions," Lucy whispered.

"No." Dee shook his head vehemently. "There have to be laws."

"Magic," Lucy breathed.

Dee just shook his head again as he fingered the woolen blanket. Then he pulled his notebook and pencil from his pocket and began to furiously record his observations. Once he had enough observations, the laws would start to become clear, he was sure of that.

Sort of.

Ai and Zi folded their legs under them as they lay down. "You may curl up against us, we will keep you warm and safe."

Cuddled up against Zi, the grass beneath him springy and soft, Dee listened to the sounds rising around him as the sky darkened. The hum of insects, the shriek of a night bird, and the croaking of frogs all combined to make a night music.

Stars began to wink into focus above him. It was so dark now, darker than it ever got in the city, that the stars seemed three-dimensional, stretching back into an unimaginable distance. He sat up with a start.

"Lucy," he whispered. "Lucy, are you awake?"

"I am now," she murmured. "What's up?"

"Lucy, the stars are all wrong."

"Wha—?"

"The constellations. I don't recognize any of them."

He heard a rustle as Lucy sat up.

"Curiouser and curiouser," she said. "I wonder how far that portal actually took us? But I doubt we'll find out soon." She rolled over and her blanket rustled as she pulled it closer around her. "So go to sleep. Who knows what tomorrow will bring?"

Dee could see the sense in that, but he was sure he wouldn't sleep a wink now. He wished he had his star charts with him. Then he might be able to figure out where they were.

The next thing he knew, Lucy was shaking his shoulder and

shouting something at him. He cracked open one eye to note the sun was now streaming through the branches. He sat up and yawned. "What? Why are you shouting at me?"

"Dee! Look!" Lucy pointed as a brilliant red and gold bird flashed from tree to tree far above them. "It looks like the same bird we saw in the woods."

Ai stood with a startled cry that sent Lucy flying.

She leaped up and clutched the Xamu's neck. "What is it, Ai? What's wrong?"

The Xamu was silent. He just stood there breathing heavily.

"Is it something about that bird?"

Ai nodded.

"Well," Lucy said, struggling to tamp down her impatience. "Out with it. What's so special about that bird?"

"It's Shuka," Zi said.

"You don't sound like you approve," Lucy tried to joke.

Dee couldn't see what all the fuss was about. Sure, the bird was terrifically beautiful, but it wasn't frightening.

Shuka flickered for an instant and then disappeared. A lone feather drifted down to land softly in the dust just ahead of Ai's front hooves.

"Oh, she's gone." Lucy sounded disappointed as she walked around Ai and stooped to pick up the feather.

Her fingers touched it and surprise flashed across her features. She drew back as if burnt, but the feather seemed to exert a strong pull that drew her back to it. She picked it up.

"What is it?" Dee asked.

"That was so weird," Lucy transferred the feather to her left hand and shook out her right. "First my palms prickled, then a tingling ran up my arm and around my throat." She touched the back of her neck. "And all the hairs on the back of my neck went up."

The feather was very long, and Dee wondered where she was going to put it. Even as he had the thought, the feather shrank until it was the perfect size to stow in the pocket of her shorts.

"You were very lucky to see her," Ai said.

"But you never know when she will show up or leave you." Zi finished for him.

"She showed us the way here," Dee said.

"I daresay she did." Ai sounded grim. "I suppose she didn't trust us to find you without her interference."

"She left you a feather." Zi sounded awed. "Some say that if you have one of Shuka's feathers, she will come to your aid."

"If she feels like it." Ai snorted.

Lucy stroked the soft feather against her cheek. It still glowed with an eerie light. "Dee, we'd better start marking the path we're taking. That will make it super easy to find our way back," she added, carefully putting the feather in the pocket of her shorts.

"Careful with that feather," Ai sounded cross. "Shuka is fickle, like Lady Luck in your world. And you never know when Lady Luck might burn you."

Lucy rolled her eyes. "Dee, do you have anything in that fancy lab coat of yours to write with? A pen? Markers?"

Dee patted his pockets and shook his head. "I just have my pencil."

"Do you have anything to make a permanent ink then?" Lucy persisted.

"Why do you want ink?" he asked.

"To mark the trees, of course. Basic survival practice for explorers." Lucy's curls bobbed as she nodded her head. "And your pencil is too close to the color of the tree trunks to be of much help."

Dee opened his lab coat and ran his fingers along the rows of little bottles. "I think I have just the thing here." He pulled out a few bottles. "Here's powdered cobalt, oil of lavender, and—do you want blue-black ink or vermillion?"

"Oh, vermillion, please!" Lucy said. "It might please Shuka. You can never have too much good fortune on your side!"

Dee nodded and selected a small jar of vermillion powder. "Now," he muttered, "I just need some water . . ."

"There's a small stream over there. Will that do?" Ai said.

Dee nodded to the Xamu. "Thank you." He handed Lucy a vial. "Go and fill this up."

When she returned, he selected an empty vial from another loop. He eyed the amount of powder as he slowly tipped some into the glass tube. He hoped this worked. He was used to measuring his ingredients precisely and he wasn't entirely comfortable just winging it. Still, it was a good idea to mark the trees.

He stoppered the vial and shook it to thoroughly mix the powder into the water. A few minutes later, he had produced a thick, brilliant red ink.

He eyeballed the result. *That should do it*, he thought.

He pulled a dropper out of another interior pocket. "We don't have any brushes, but we can use this to drop ink onto the bark of trees to mark our way."

Lucy stepped up to the nearest tree and let several beads of the brilliant fluid fall on the trunk. A vivid vermillion streak glistened in the sunshine.

"Awesome, Dee. Now we will be able to retrace our steps."

"I certainly hope so." Dee cast a longing glance back toward the mouth of the tunnel.

"What could go wrong?" Lucy snorted. "The mark is blazingly obvious."

If it doesn't get washed away by a rainstorm, rubbed off by an animal brushing against the bark, or go up in flames in a fire, Dee thought.

"Now let's get going." Lucy headed for Ai and prepared to mount.

From that point on, the Xami stopped every hundred feet so that she could mark their way until, several hours later, they stopped.

CHAPTER SIX

"We had better …" said Ai.

"Stop here," said Zi.

"What is this place?" Lucy indicated the roadside stand that had appeared when they'd went around a curve in the road. Behind it stretched a field laid out with neat rows of low glass tanks filled with dirt.

"We need to pay a visit to the word wrangler."

"You mean a worm wrangler," Lucy corrected him as she looked at the tanks.

"No, we mean …" said Zi.

"A word wrangler," finished Ai.

"Why do we need a word wrangler?" Lucy wondered.

"Do you speak Sericean?" Ai inquired.

Lucy opened her mouth and then shut it again.

"We thought not." Ai sounded smug. "The word wrangler trains worms to translate words. And here is T now."

A tall, skinny man wearing brown overalls and a green shirt walked toward them with a rolling gait. As he approached the Xami, he bowed his head in respect. "Serene Ones."

When he straightened, he looked at Dee and Lucy and said, "Gracious Lord, Gracious Lady, my name is T and I'm very pleased to meet you." He held out his hand and gravely shook hands with the children.

Then he turned back to the Xami. "How can I help you today, Serene Ones?"

"We are looking for two pairs of translator worms, T," said Ai.

"Well, you've come to the right place then." T's eyelids crinkled at the corners as his lips curved into a broad smile. "Are you ready to pick yours, Gracious Lady?"

"Yes," replied Lucy after a moment, still taken aback at being called Gracious Lady.

"And you, Gracious Lord?"

Dee's mouth went down at the corners. "Absolutely not. Definitely, NO!"

Lucy knew that Dee wasn't afraid of many things, but spiders and small wriggly things that lived under rocks gave him the screaming horrors. He'd always been clear he wasn't going to be an entomologist when he grew up.

T glanced at Dee. "Well, you're going to find it mighty difficult here without one," he mused. "I was in a right mess here until I discovered these little beauties." Then he shrugged. "But that's entirely your choice of course."

T set off at a brisk pace and Lucy had to trot to keep up with him. Dee hesitated a moment and then broke into an ungainly lope behind Lucy. She smiled to herself. She didn't think he'd want to be left behind.

Her head whipped to the left and right as they passed many different tanks, each with a placard illustrating the type of worms it held plus a description.

"There are many different people who travel this road. And they speak countless different languages. Or at least they used to before *she* arrived in the Celestial City. It's been ages since we've seen anyone new," T explained. "Word is she's closing off all the entry points." T scowled.

He gave his head a little shake and forced a smile as he continued his explanation. "So, this tank of worms can translate Russian into Sericean and vice versa." He gestured to a long, low tank on their left.

"And this one," he pointed to a tall, narrow tank on their right. "Translates between Italian and Sericean and so on and so forth. You want tank number seventy-six, the red wiggler worm. It will translate the words you hear into English and the words that you want to speak into Sericean."

T put on gloves. "This is so I don't contaminate the soil. Diseases can spread like wildfire and wipe out an entire tank whether it's plants, animals, or a mixture," he explained, looking at Lucy's puzzled face. Then he dug around in the tank and lifted four worms out of their moist dark home and into the bright sunlight. They curled away protectively trying to hide behind each other. "Hold your hands out now."

Lucy thrust her hand forward. "How do they work?"

"You have to drop one in each ear." T dropped two of the worms into Lucy's outstretched hand. Beside her, Dee gave a squawk of dismay and stuck his hands behind his back.

"You do it," Lucy said to T. She handed the worms back to T as she used her free hand to pull her hair back and away from her ears.

Deftly, he dropped a worm into each ear. Lucy shuddered. The worms tickled for a moment and then the sensation went away.

"C'mon, Dee. It doesn't hurt. It just tickles for a minute. Try it. What could go wrong?"

Dee looked at her in amazement. "You know how I feel about creepy-crawlies, and you ask me that?"

Lucy waved a dismissive hand. "Oh, please. Don't use your bitter voice with me. Seriously, think about how much trouble we could get into if we don't understand what's going on around us. It could be dangerous." She let her voice drop on the last word. "I promise you won't even feel them after a few seconds. Trust me."

"Oh, for Pete's sake," Dee muttered and held out his hand. "Could I see one, please?"

"Sure," T dropped one into Dee's outstretched palm.

Dee carefully examined the reddish-brown creature. It was about four inches long but only about a quarter inch in diameter.

"Does it do anything else?" Dee looked up at T.

"Sure does. It gives a different signal to your brain to help your mouth form the Sericean words. You can understand the language and you can also speak it."

"Okay, definitely going to be essential." Dee caved in and submitted to having the worms inserted with only a few faint yelps and shudders.

When T finished, he added, "And if you don't need it for translating, it can create compost in your garden."

Dee said, "Translator worms are interesting creatures."

"I have all sorts of interesting things here. I'm an inventor, you know," said T.

Dee perked up. "What else have you invented?"

"Well, see here?" He led them over to a row of cages. "Here I have what you might call a dragon whisperer." He pulled a small furry creature out of a nearby cage.

"Looks like an ordinary hedgehog to me," Lucy said.

"No, Gracious Lady. Not an ordinary hedgehog. This one, if you squeeze it in just the right spot, will summon the most powerful dragons known to human and beast."

Dee's eyes gleamed with a strange light. "How much do you want for it?"

"Well now, I don't rightly know," T stroked his chin. "What have you got to offer me?"

Dee fished around in his pocket. He weighed the octant thoughtfully in his hand for a moment and then appeared to come to a decision. "This." He held it up.

"Dee, are you nuts!" Lucy almost shrieked as she stepped toward him to pull him away from the word wrangler. *What does he think he's doing?*

Dee waved Lucy away and looked expectantly at T.

"That's a mighty fine-looking device you have there," T said. "I think it's worth this young fellow in exchange."

Dee stretched out his other hand for the dragon whisperer and then dropped the octant into T's now empty hand. Dee's smile broadened as he looked at the small animal.

"But—" objected Lucy.

Dee shushed her before saying, "Thank you so much for your time, T. We appreciate your help. We will say goodbye now."

"Yes, thanks, T. Thanks for the translator worms. Bye!" Lucy gave the word wrangler a little wave. She and Dee turned to leave. "But no thanks for scamming Dee with a sketchy hedgehog," she scowled, muttering under her breath as they walked away.

Once they were out of earshot of the word wrangler, she turned on him. "How could you do that? You said we needed the octant to get home again. And it belonged to your uncle!"

"We've marked the trees, Lucy. Remember? That was your bright idea. And my uncle would have supported trading it in the spirit of inquiry. Don't you realize that we have now come across four new species if you count Lord Petram. I'd have been silly to give up an opportunity to examine a dragon whisperer."

"But . . ." Lucy didn't know what to say. Sure, she'd figured marking the trees was a good idea, but still, they had to be able to find the Silk Road again.

"I've always wanted a dragon," Dee said firmly. "Dragons are supposed to be one of the most powerful creatures. They aren't afraid of anything."

"In mythology, Dee! Not in the real world."

"You mean not in *our* world. But we're not in our world anymore, are we, Lucy? Who knows what other strange and marvelous creatures live here?" Dee's chin jutted out with defiance. "I am going to call this little fellow Bertie."

He stroked the little beast. It looked up at him and blinked beady black eyes.

"He is kind of cute," she said, softening slightly as she reached out to gently touch the top of Bertie's head.

"Besides"—Dee looked her straight in the eye—"as you say, what could go wrong?"

"What could go wrong!" Lucy's voice rose to a shriek. She stomped on ahead of Dee and put her forehead on Ai's flank. "What do we do now?"

"Fulfill your quest here," said Ai. "That's the only way you'll find Shuka again. She will lead you home when your mission is complete."

A short while later, they came out of the forest to see fields stretching far into the distance.

"Now we are taking you to the Celestial City," said Zi as they turned off the Silk Road to join a much larger roadway constructed with thick paving stones.

"Welcome to the Imperial Way," said Zi. "It is the lifeblood of Sericea."

Traffic increased as they joined camels, caravans, overburdened donkeys, and laden carts all moving in the same direction. The honks and bellows of the animals mingled with the cries and curses of the men and women driving or walking along beside them.

There were cries of "Make way" as the wealthy, in covered and curtained palanquins, pushed their way through the throngs of animals and traders. Farmers bent under baskets brimming with fresh produce of every kind. Clusters of people in tattered clothes trailed along the side of the road on dirty bare feet lugging their few possessions in a sack on their back or pushing them in a small barrow. Occasionally they held out a hand, their eyes dull and hopeless as they begged for alms.

Lucy wished she had some money or had kept some food, anything to make these poor travelers' journeys a little easier.

The sun burned and it seemed to Lucy that their journey would never end. Her eyes drooped as a wave of fatigue washed over her, but still the Xami trotted along the roadway. Despite the activity around her, she had almost dozed off when Ai stumbled. Lucy jerked forward, hitting her nose with a sharp bump on the back of his neck.

Wide awake now, she sat up and surveyed her surroundings as she rubbed her throbbing nose. Men and women wearing baggy black pants, loose black shirts, and woven, broad-brimmed hats, stooped as they dug into the earth with hoes. After a while, Lucy realized there was something odd about their grouping. There would be about a dozen people clumped together with one person carrying a large whip following them on a horse. A little further away would be a similar grouping. She sat up straight and shaded her eyes with her hand.

"Ai?" Her tone was sharp. "Are those people chained together?"

Ai nodded.

A whip cracked through the air. One of the prisoners sank to his knees with a cry only to be struck by the whip again and again until he got to his feet. Lucy shut her eyes to the horror.

"Why?" she whispered.

"So they don't run away," Ai replied.

"Well, duh!" Lucy huffed. "But why are there chain gangs at all? I thought you said that the emperor ensured unity for all under heaven."

"He did," Zi chimed in. "But unity doesn't mean equality. It means all the little kingdoms have been made one under one rule. But the chain gangs are new. And they don't bode well for continued peaceful rule."

"You said it," Dee agreed, pulling a small telescope from one of the pockets in his lab coat and scanning the field. He replaced the telescope and, looking thoughtful, dipped his hand in his other pocket and took out Bertie. "We're going to have to find you something to eat and drink soon, aren't we?" He stroked the little creature and it snuggled contentedly in the palm of his hand.

The mention of food had Lucy's stomach grumbling and she realized that it had been a long time since their dinner with Lord Petram. She sighed as she scanned the road ahead. There wasn't a restaurant to be seen. It looked like it would be quite some time before her next meal. She looked out over the fields again. Who knew what those poor souls were getting to eat?

"Ai, it's awful that these people are chained and whipped. What kind of place is this, really?" she said.

The Xamu just kept steadily moving along the road.

"Why would anyone force people to work like that?" Dee asked. "Are they slaves or prisoners? We used to have prison gangs where we come from but not anymore. Whatever the reason, I don't like it one bit."

"Ai," Lucy buried her fingers in Ai's ruff for comfort. "If our mission goes wrong, could we end up in one of those chain gangs?" A headache began right between her eyebrows.

"And why doesn't the emperor do something about them? What kind of monster is he?" Dee burst out. "Or is he in danger of ending up in chains too?"

"The emperor is young," Zi continued. "And unable to do much about the plight of his people. The one who is really in charge is taking a harsh line with anyone who speaks out against her."

"But—"

"It's best we don't discuss it any further." Zi cut Lucy off. "You will soon see for yourselves."

Dee put Bertie back in his pocket and gathered Zi's reins in his hands again. "I wonder what we're in for now," he said, turning to Lucy.

She just shrugged, her eyes fixed on the road ahead.

CHAPTER SEVEN

By midafternoon, a broad river stretched before them. In front of the children ran a long quay. Another one mirrored it on the other side of the river. Dee watched as burly men scurried like ants loading and unloading cargo from boats and carts. Ships and other watercraft of all sizes bustled between the two shores. Past the opposite docks rose a hill.

He looked up. A high stone wall ran around the top. In the center of the wall, enormous iron gates yawned open beyond which the tips of spires glinted gold and silver in the sunlight.

Ai stopped and sang out. A boatman ran up to them and, skidding to a stop in front of the Xami, dropped into a deep bow. "Yes, Serene Ones?"

"We need passage across," Zi stated.

"Immediately, Serene Ones." The boatman backed away, still bowing. Then he straightened and beckoned them to follow him. "My vessel is just here."

The Xami followed, and Dee swayed from side to side as Zi stepped, daintily for such a large creature, down the slope, across the dock, and onto the deck of the flat-bottomed boat.

The boatman cast off and pulled a long pole from a holder. Planting his feet firmly on the deck he plunged the pole into the water and pushed them off the bank.

The Xami folded themselves into a kneeling position and the

children slid off. Lucy sat with her back against the railing and, eyes closed, lifted her face to the sunlight.

Dee took Bertie out of his pocket and let him nose around on the deck. He stroked the little creature with one gentle finger.

A few minutes later, Dee leaned over the edge. "Lucy, look here! I've never seen water this pure." He scooped some water into the palm of his hand and let Bertie drink from it.

Black and silver fish darted among the water grasses. A bright green beetle scuttled along the riverbed, diving into the sand as the shadow of the boat passed overhead. A warm breeze ruffled Dee's hair and he briefly enjoyed the moment. Then he fished his notebook and pencil out of his pocket and began to note his observations.

The broad river was busy with river craft of all sizes. Fishermen brought wide flat baskets heaped with silvery fish. Dee wondered how many new species of fish there were in this strange place. He tried sketching a few of them but was soon frustrated by his limited artistic capabilities. "Really?" he muttered to himself. "How hard is it to draw a fish?" He tore the page out of his notebook and crumpled it up. A moment later he smoothed it out and tucked it back in the book.

Many fishing boats had large birds sitting on the prow of the boat. Dee remembered a fun fact from one of his favorite nature programs: the diving birds used by fishermen all had rings around their necks so they couldn't swallow the large fish they caught.

Long broad barges were heaped with grain, some golden, some white, and some brown. Other boats seemed to be a ferry service, like the one he was on, taking traders and travelers to and from the city. One ship, currently moored, soared above the rest. It was much longer than any of the others and topped with an ornately decorated structure covering the deck. Its intricate paneling, vibrant colors, and painted decorations told Dee this was the vessel of a very important person. He pointed to the pennant, vibrant royal blue with a gold dragon centered on it, fluttering above the main sail. "Do you know who owns this boat, Zi?"

The Xamu turned his head to look. "That's the imperial barge. The blue and gold are the royal colors."

Dee saw Lucy staring at the boat. Was she wondering the same thing he was? Did the emperor use his barge regularly? Did he get out and see his subjects? Did he know about the chain gangs and just not care? Dee furrowed his brow. If the emperor was that sort of person, Dee wondered how he could befriend him. *Maybe this is why the emperor doesn't have any friends*, he thought. *Maybe he just isn't a very nice person*. Dee's heart sank at the prospect.

His reverie was broken when, with a small bump, the boat came to a dock on the other side of the river. He scooped Bertie up from the deck, slipped him back in his pocket, and rose to his feet.

The boatman grabbed a coil of rope and jumped onto the dock, rapidly twisting the rope around a post to secure the boat. Then he held out a hand to help first Lucy and then Dee step onto the boards.

Once on solid land, Dee looked at the surrounding activity. A long cavalcade of carts pulled by mules wound its way up the slope and disappeared into the enclosure behind the main city gates.

The Xami stopped just behind him.

"Behold, the Celestial City," Zi said with a flourish of his right front leg.

The children remounted and the Xami pranced, heads and tails held high, up the wide stone-paved road and through the towering gates. The city spread out from the main thoroughfare. On the outermost rim, closest to the walls, small three- or four-story buildings were jumbled together. At street level, bright red banners crisscrossed the road advertising various shops and their wares: food, leather goods, drinks, household goods, and clothes. Many of these items sat arranged in baskets on tiered stands outside the front doors of the shops. Shopkeepers stood in their doorways gossiping with their customers. A troupe of actors stopped their impromptu street corner performance to turn and stare.

The smells of cooking, animals, pyramids of spices, and fresh fruit, all overlayed with the odor of many people living close together, swirled through the air.

At the sight of the Xami, everyone took a step back and bowed their heads. When they looked up again, they gawked at the children riding on the Xami's backs. "This feels a little awkward," Lucy murmured to Dee.

He nodded as he shifted uncomfortably on Zi's back. He had never liked being the center of attention.

The windows of the upper floors of the buildings had been flung open and brightly colored curtains fluttered above window boxes filled with flowers. Narrow, twisting streets spun off the main road in all directions and people hurried along, clutching purchases in one hand and, often, a small protesting child in the other.

Dee widened his eyes, but no matter how hard he tried he just couldn't take it all in. There was too much color, too many scents from the food stalls, and over it all rose the chatter of the people.

Everywhere he looked, someone was staring open-mouthed at the two children riding the magnificent Xami.

A vendor with a tray slung around his neck, stepped out in front of them. "Gracious Lady, Gracious Lord, may I offer you a delicacy from my selection?" A gold tooth twinkled as the man spoke.

Dee looked at the contents of the vendor's tray and his mouth watered. There were small cakes covered with candied fruit and honey, round cookies studded with nuts and spices, and pastries that sparkled with crystals of sugar. What really caught his eye, though, were the long twists of pastry covered in powdered sugar.

He patted the pockets of his lab coat, not sure what he expected to find there. He knew he didn't have any Sericean money but still found himself inexplicably disappointed when he didn't find any in his pockets.

"I'm sorry," he shook his head. "I can't pay for anything."

"No, no, Gracious Lord," the vendor stepped back holding his hand up. "You misunderstand me. I mean it as a gift." He smiled at them.

"Zi?" Dee murmured.

The Xamu bobbed his head. "It is safe, Dee. Please accept his kind gift. The man would be embarrassed if you refused." He rolled his eyes to indicate the gathering crowd.

After a certain amount of hesitation and hemming and hawing,

Lucy chose a cream-filled cake covered with candied apricots and Dee snapped off the end of the pastry stick he'd been eyeing hungrily.

The children thanked the vendor, and the little procession continued uphill. Dee looked back to see the vendor mobbed by curious townspeople wondering who the children were and what they were doing there.

A little snout poked out from Dee's pocket, the black tip of its nose twitching at the scent of the food. Dee broke off a piece of his pastry and fed it to Bertie. He would have to find some food more suitable for the dragon whisperer once he figured out what that might be.

Dee finished the rest of the pastry and wished he had another. He pointed with a forefinger still covered in powdered sugar so Lucy would look up. The gold and silver spires were closer now. As the road curled and twisted around the hill, they appeared and disappeared but were larger at each sighting.

"How far are we from the Imperial Palace now, Zi?" Dee asked as curiosity warred with nervousness.

"Not far, about twenty minutes." The Xamu bobbed his head gently as he pranced up the winding roadway.

Dee's stomach clenched as he wondered who and what they would encounter when they arrived. Would the danger become obvious immediately or would it take time to reveal itself? He looked all around, squinting at the road and surrounding buildings for a lurking shadow.

As they went deeper and higher into the city, the buildings became bigger and grander. No longer were there shops on the ground level of the houses, and soon the homes disappeared behind stone walls and extensive gardens. These were clearly the mansions of the wealthy. The only sounds were the hooves of the Xami on the stone road, the songs of birds, and the children's breathing.

That made sense, Dee thought. When Aunt Delia had taken him to Prague last summer, they had seen Prague Castle at the top of the hill and the mansions of former nobles and high government officials downhill. Aunt Delia said the placement of the mansions was to show the nobles' inferior position to the Bohemian King while keeping them nearby to be close to the court. It looked like the Sericeans had the same system. But just to be sure ...

"Do the princes and high officials live in these houses, Zi?"

The Xamu nodded. "But most of them are the same people—the aristocrats hold all the high positions."

Now Dee could see the red and gold roofs supporting the glittering spires of the magnificent structure at the top of the hill.

One last curve in the road and the Imperial Palace spread out in all its glory. Dee gasped. Before them, the road straightened. Stationed along the sides were creatures that looked like a cross between lions and dogs. They sat on their haunches and their red eyes glowed with watchfulness as the Xami and the children approached.

Muscles, big muscles, rippled along its flanks as one of the creatures shifted position slightly. One by one the creatures stood, alert now. Dee glimpsed flashes of white as black lips drew back to reveal silvery white fangs.

Fear rippled up his back and Dee's grip tightened on the reins. He leaned forward, about to ask Zi to turn around, when the Xami stopped and opened their mouths.

The same beautiful music that Dee had heard in the tunnel poured now from their throats and the giant guard creatures seemed to softly sigh in unison. Then they sagged and folded themselves onto the ground in a submissive position. Dee hummed the music quietly to himself.

With a toss of his head, Zi moved forward again as Ai kept up the brisk pace beside him. Lucy smiled broadly and gave Dee a thumbs-up. Slowly and carefully, Dee let out the breath he'd been holding.

"That was terrifying," he muttered. "What kind of creatures are those monsters?"

"They are called the Guardians, for obvious reasons," Zi said as he trotted up the road.

Lucy looked back at the line of beasts. "There you go, Dee. Another species for your list of new and fabulous creatures."

Dee shook his head. Did nothing faze that girl?

Moments later, the road ended in a massive courtyard. It was the size of a football field and teeming with people, palanquins, carts, and animals.

A path opened before the Xami as they continued their stately approach to the palace.

At the far end of the courtyard, a broad staircase rose to the entrance. Immense, shiny red doors with golden designs stood shut fast against the children. On either side, guards held lances tipped with wicked looking spikes. Dee's heart hammered in his throat, and he began to wonder if this was where things would go wrong. His hand shook as he stroked Zi's neck for comfort. The Xamu bobbed his head as if to acknowledge his nervousness and reassure him at the same time.

Once again, the Xami sang, and as the doors swung open, the guards stepped back and bowed low. The Xami's hooves clicked on the floor as they made their way into the interior, and Dee had to blink as his eyes adjusted to the dim light. As the Xami moved purposefully toward an interior chamber, he noted dark red walls covered in paintings and a black floor so shiny that he could see their reflections in it. Statues sat upon plinths that were covered with decorative jade carvings of sinuous dragons and stalking lions. Vases made of alabaster and decorated with precious stones sat on small, lacquered tables scattered around the chamber. Above, a dome soared into the heavens, and in the center a circular skylight set deep into the cupola admitted daylight, filling the room with a soft glow. A bell rang in the distance. The room was large enough for hundreds, but there were no other people here.

"Wow," Dee muttered under his breath. "Hey Lucy, want to hear a fun architectural fact?" He didn't wait for her response. "That dome is probably an inner dome. Between it and the outer dome must be some kind of ring of heavy ribs to support the whole structure." The sheer magnificence of the interior of the palace was overwhelming.

"Uh-huh." Lucy's head swiveled to the left and right. "Wait! What did you just do?" she finally asked. "It sounded like your voice came from over there?" She pointed to the other side of the dome.

"Some domes have strange acoustic effects, known as whispering-gallery waves, and project sounds to a distance. But you have to be standing in just the right spot." Dee explained. "Some caves have the same effect."

Lucy smiled. "Fascinating."

Dee tucked his chin, looked down, and smiled.

Two enormous urns, made from a blue stone so thin it was almost transparent, flanked the doorway to the interior chamber. As the children passed through, a guard poked his head out from behind the right-hand urn and stopped them.

"State your business!"

"The children are guests of the Emperor Yidi," Ai said.

"Guests?" The guard pulled a rustling sheaf of paper from his pocket. "Names?" He gave Lucy and Dee a hard look.

Lucy took a deep breath. "Well, I'm Lucy Banks."

"And I'm Dee Ringrose." It came out as a strangled croak. Were they going to be turned back now, when they were so close to reaching the emperor?

The guard rustled his papers again and his lips moved as his gaze scanned the written characters. Dee held his breath. He wondered if Zi had told the guard a whopping great lie, because no one had told him that the emperor had invited them. This guard looked cranky and the sword at his side looked mighty sharp.

The guard's lips moved some more as he turned the first page over and ran his finger down the text. "Ah, yes, here you are." He sounded disappointed. Dee figured that carving them up would have been the most exciting thing to happen to him in a long time. But he drew a sigh of relief as the guard pushed open the door and made an abrupt motion. "Go on then. Enter. The emperor awaits you."

CHAPTER EIGHT

The first things Lucy noticed were the noises and the smells. Unlike the outer chamber, this room was crowded with people and their chatter rose to the ceiling along with thick curls of incense rising from sticky looking brown cones in glazed bowls. Flowers filled brilliantly colored vases placed on tables made of glowing wood inlaid with precious stones.

Guards in royal blue and gold headdresses were spaced evenly around the perimeter of the room. They wore armbands featuring a gold dragon motif, and long curved swords rested at their waists.

Groups of men and women dressed in long silk robes in all the colors of the rainbow paused in their conversations to turn to stare at the new arrivals. They grew silent as they recognized the Xami and stepped back on feet shod in elaborately embroidered slippers.

Prickles, sharp as tiny electric shocks traveled up and down Lucy's spine.

The crowd retreated further, and a pathway opened to the end of the vast chamber.

Lucy looked down the long line of people now flanking the path. At the very end was a platform made of the same shiny black wood. On it sat two large chairs intricately carved and covered in gold. In one chair slouched a round figure, but it was the woman who stood behind the chair that caught Lucy's attention.

She was tall, the tallest woman that Lucy had ever seen, with blond hair that fell straight to her waist. Unlike the others in the room, who had various shades of brown skin, like the townspeople, she was strikingly pale. She wore a simple white robe, pleated from the shoulder, and cinched around her waist with a golden sash. It fell to the floor where it ended in a royal blue fringe. Her arms were bare and she wore thick gold cuffs on her wrists. A large blue stone was centered on each cuff.

"Blue opal," Dee murmured in response to Lucy's raised eyebrow as she stared at the glowing blue stones.

But it was the magnificent necklace she wore that next drew Lucy's gaze. A large golden pectoral medallion with a huge tiger's eye in the middle hung from a thick strand of twisted gold. The woman looked astonished to see them, and not particularly pleased. She reached up to touch her medallion.

An enormous tiger wearing a jeweled collar sprawled at her feet. He slit open one golden eye and focused on Lucy. Stretching one foreleg, he flexed his paw and extended sharp claws.

The Xami kept up their dignified approach to the platform, the sharp staccato sounds of their hooves explosive in the thick silence. Lucy found that she was no more capable of leaving the throne room than she was of sprouting wings.

The little group drew to a stop in front of the platform and the Xami bowed over their extended right legs.

At a short command from Zi, Lucy and Dee clambered down.

"Kneel," Ai hissed. "And bow. Your foreheads must touch the floor."

"What?" said Lucy in a loud, indignant voice. "Nobody kneels for anyone where I come from."

"Lucy, *kneel!*" There was a hint of desperation in Ai's voice now. Lucy could hear the sharp tap of the woman's pointed nails on the back of the throne. Looking sideways, Lucy saw Dee sink gracefully to his knees, then his haunches and finally bow, arms outstretched before him.

Lucy hesitated. This felt wrong ... demeaning.

Zi stamped his foot as the scrape of a sword being released from its scabbard rasped along Lucy's nerves. "Do you want to lose your head, child?"

The guard with the sword muttered, "Get on with it, kid." He lifted his weapon.

Lucy did *not* want to lose her head. Thinking so fast her thoughts had no time to wave to her as they sped by, she prostrated herself. "Ouch," she muttered as her kneecap banged on the hard marble floor.

Ai addressed the figure in the chair and the imperious woman beside it in turn. "Holy Majesty, Great Mother Queen Xixi—"

"Why have you brought these small barbarians into this most sacred space?" interrupted the queen. "Into the presence of the emperor?" She put her hand on the slouching figure.

That's the emperor? Lucy lifted her head a bit and stared in amazement. The guard next to her hissed and from the corner of her eye, Lucy saw the sharp tip of his sword twitch. She put her head down again.

"We have brought these children to meet His Holy Majesty, Emperor Yidi." The Xami said in unison.

Flames appeared to ripple over and around the Xami, but Lucy felt no heat from them. Another gasp arose from the crowd.

"These children will stay to provide companionship to him, and they are under our protection." The Xami spoke in unison in tones as thunderous as church bells.

Okaaaaaay, thought Lucy. *At least they're making it clear they'll be keeping an eye on us.*

For one moment, Queen Xixi looked uncertain and took a step back.

The tiger sat up now. Seated, his great head came to the queen's shoulder. He yawned, exposing a long red tongue and glistening white fangs. Lucy tried to make herself as small as possible.

"You are right to be afraid, little barbarian," the queen drawled. "Sabu would tear you apart in an instant should I allow him to do so."

As if in agreement, the tiger emitted a low rumbling growl as his tail lashed the floor.

Then the queen pointed a long, white finger at Lucy and Dee. "Who are you?"

"I am Lucy Banks, your Majesty." Lucy risked another glance at the queen and saw her press her lips together in irritation.

"And you, boy?"

"I-I-I ..." Dee tried to choke the words out and his face reddened to almost the same color as his hair. "D-d-d—"

"Oh, please!" The queen flapped her hand at him and turned away from him.

Dee pillowed his head in his arms and his back quivered. Lucy made a small sympathetic sound. Dee didn't stutter often now, only when he was very stressed, and even then, it didn't bother him too much. She remembered him telling her once that Charles Darwin had stuttered, and it hadn't slowed *him* down.

"These children aren't worthy of meeting the emperor." A figure Lucy hadn't noticed before now spoke. He was a tall portly man, although not as tall as the queen, and it looked like a badger had collapsed on his head before death overtook it.

He looks ridiculous, Lucy thought, daring to lift her head slightly to take a quick peek. The tip of the guard's blade touched the side of her throat and she stilled, instantly.

"Do they come from noble blood? I don't think so," the man answered his own question. "Holy Majesty needs no other companionship." He gestured at the slouched form of the boy on the throne. The boy barely glanced at Lucy before looking away. "Not when he has me to guide him. After all, how could they possibly have anything to offer," the man went on, puffing up his chest. "I am the smartest man in the kingdom and can give the young emperor all of the answers he needs. No, these children need to be escorted back to where they belong before they pollute our society." He folded his hands inside his sleeves and stuck both his chins out.

A rumble of approval came from behind him. "Probably criminals," came muttered agreement.

It was only then Lucy noticed that several other people, all richly dressed, hovered behind the throne. Their gazes were unfriendly.

"Shush, fool, we can discuss this later," hissed the queen. A mottled flush spread up her neck and across her cheeks as her eyes narrowed. "At the moment, this is out of our hands." She didn't sound at all happy about it.

There was silence as the queen seemed to be thinking something through. Then a remarkable change came over her and she smiled at Lucy and Dee.

"Forgive me." She stepped forward and gracefully sank into the chair beside the emperor's before stretching her hands out to Lucy and Dee. "Come here. Let me get a better look at you."

Lucy looked to Ai for confirmation. She really didn't want to lose her head, and the man with the sword had been serious. The Xamu nodded, his scales shimmering, and took several steps back.

Lucy and Dee scrambled to their feet.

"Come, come, now." The queen smiled again, and Lucy thought that it completely transformed her. Now the woman radiated kindness and interest.

"I can see that I must have sounded a bit abrupt and unfriendly. Your arrival surprised me, that's all." The queen said in a voice that was suddenly low and musical. "The Xami rarely grace us with their presence." All traces of her previous harshness had disappeared. "Don't worry, no one here is going to harm you." She waved a slim white hand to encompass the room.

"Let's start again," the queen suggested. "Come and sit here, beside me."

She motioned to two attendants hovering in the background. Immediately, they rushed forward with two more chairs.

"Now, you look much more comfortable. Since you've arrived here, and are under the protection of the Xami, I think it's best we get to know each other a bit better, don't you? But first, you must be hungry and thirsty after your journey." Xixi gestured to another attendant who rushed forward. The queen whispered some instructions and the servant scampered off.

Lucy's gaze was drawn again to the spectacular medallion. Strange symbols surrounded the tiger's eye with three of the symbols on what would be ten o'clock, twelve o'clock, and two o'clock. The queen reached up to touch it again. "Yes, it's a very special piece," she said.

Lucy nodded and managed to take her gaze from it as the servant returned with a silver tray mounded with pastries dripping with honey and two silver goblets containing a sparkly pink liquid.

Lucy took the goblet that the attendant offered her and, taking a cautious sniff of the liquid, found that it smelled like raspberries. Reassured, she took a sip and smiled as it burst in bright bubbles along her tongue.

"And a small cake, perhaps?" The queen held out the tray of pastries.

The boy emperor glanced at the queen and raised an eyebrow. But he didn't stir any further.

Lucy, relieved the queen wasn't going to have her head removed from her shoulders, took a big pastry and crammed it in her mouth. She paused after swallowing it. It had a peculiar aftertaste. Still, she imagined the pastries here might be made with different spices. *But the pastry in the town didn't have a funny aftertaste*, a small voice inside her said.

A warm glow spread through Lucy, and she ignored the small, treacherous voice. But she noticed that Dee hadn't touched the food, not even to give Bertie a few crumbs.

CHAPTER NINE

"**N**ow," said the queen. Her green eyes sparkled, and she seemed to be settling in for a cozy chat. "I'm curious. How did you manage to find Sericea? It has been several years since we received our last two barbarian guests. And they were adults, not charming children like you two. Was it difficult for you to find your way?"

Lucy shook her head. "Not at all. Shuka showed us the entrance to the tunnel and then Lord Petram met us and told us we had this mission to accomplish—" She broke off. "What's the matter with you?" she said to Dee. His face was strangely contorted.

The queen turned and fixed Dee with her cool gaze. "Is there something wrong, child?"

A deep flush suffused Dee's face. "Ah, I just didn't think it was necessary ... I mean, I thought we shouldn't ... maybe you should hush, Lucy!" he finished in a desperate rush. At Lucy's astonished expression, he shut his mouth and looked at the floor.

"Who is Lord Petram?" asked the queen.

Lucy felt a glow of pride. Lucy had always thought queens were supposed to know everything, but this one was asking her for answers. Lucy puffed out her chest a little. She was important. Now she wanted to tell the queen everything—show her just how much she knew.

"He's the lord of all the rock throughout the land," Lucy waved an expansive arm to illustrate. "He controls it," She added for good measure.

63

"Does he indeed?" The queen looked first impressed, then thoughtful. ·

"Anyway," Lucy continued. She was thoroughly charmed by Xixi. She never got this much attention at home except when it came to getting assigned her chores, and it encouraged her to continue her story. "We went down the tunnel and found the Silk Road. We learned about the Silk Road in school, but this was quite different." She shrugged her shoulders as if to shed this mystery. "Then the Xami galloped up, carried us through the tunnel, and then here."

"And could you find your way back to the entrance of the tunnel?" Xixi leaned forward, her chin in the palm of her hand. Her fingers, tipped with dangerously long red nails, curled pensively around her mouth.

"Sure could." Lucy continued to ignore Dee's eyebrow wiggling, as she recounted to the queen how they had marked their route with indelible ink. She was proud of that foresight.

"What puzzles me," Queen Xixi said, "is how you understand us. Surely, we don't speak the same language. The last two barbarians certainly didn't. We had a terrible time understanding them."

The boy emperor snickered.

"Oh, that was easy," Lucy flapped a careless hand. "T, he's the owner of a farm of translator worms, gave us the right ones. You just drop them in your ears"—she pulled back her hair on one side to demonstrate—"and the worms take care of the rest."

"Translator worms ... fascinating," the queen murmured. "Have another sweet cake." She gestured to the attendant to pass the silver tray around again. Lucy selected another cake.

"And this worm farm. Where is it, exactly, my dear?" the queen persisted.

Dee made frantic little signals that Lucy continued to ignore. *What's gotten into him anyhow?* she fumed. *What could go wrong? Isn't it better to be on Queen Xixi's good side?*

Lucy helped herself to another big cake. "It's not far from the entrance to the tunnel. Once we got to Sericea, we kept riding until it got dark. We slept outside and Lord Petram made us these amazing blankets. This morning, we rode to the worm farm, and it took the rest of the day to ride here." The servant filled Lucy's goblet with more of the sparkling liquid.

"It was pretty cool that we found the place," Lucy continued before taking a grateful sip. Her throat was still dry after the long ride. "Knowing the language will definitely help us here on our mission."

"Your mission?" The queen raised an eyebrow.

Lucy felt a bolt of alarm. *Why did I say that?* She tried to brush it off. "Oh, you know, like the Xami said—meet the emperor, keep him company," she blustered and then buried her nose in her goblet to avoid the queen's gaze.

When she lifted her head again, Lucy saw the queen's eyes had narrowed slightly. "I can't help but think there's more to it than just keeping His Holy Majesty company."

"We'd like to learn about Sericea. It's a new country for us. I've always wanted to have an adventure, and Dee is very interested in the scientific possibilities," Lucy said before taking a bite from the cake in her other hand.

"Still, a mission has a goal. So, what is it you're really here to do?"

She sure is insistent, Lucy thought. She squirmed slightly in her chair, but a large mouthful of cake had rendered her momentarily speechless.

"No matter, I'm sure we will discover it soon enough. But I'm not sure you know what you're getting into. I trust it won't turn out to be too dangerous." She leaned forward. A blue spark jumped between them as the queen placed a slim white hand on Lucy's arm. It was the weirdest static electricity Lucy had ever seen. The queen's skin was cold to the touch and Lucy suppressed a sudden shiver.

"I hope so too," Lucy said. Warning bells clanged again in her head, stifling her desire to tell the queen anything more.

"It would be dreadful if harm were to befall such a lovely girl as you."

Dee snorted and Lucy glared at him before turning back to Queen Xixi.

"And when you've completed this mission? Then what?" The

queen studied Lucy's face carefully. Lucy felt heat spread across her cheeks.

"Well then Lord Petram will give Dee the key to transmutation so that he can turn lead into gold, and we will search for Dee's parents." The words burst past her lips despite her best efforts to shut up, and her head felt funny.

By now, Dee had his face in his hands and was shaking his head slowly back and forth and the boy emperor was leaning forward, his eyes bright.

"Turn lead into gold. Amazing," breathed the queen. "Well, I, for one, will certainly follow your progress with considerable interest." Her eyes held a strange gleam. "You must stay as our honored guests for a good long time."

"Your Majesty, I must protest!" the tall portly man huffed.

The queen silenced him with a glance. Sabu growled.

"I know the emperor would indeed appreciate the companionship of children his age. It was kind of the Xami to bring you here," she went on, gesturing to the youth beside her. "Yidi, it's time to be sociable."

"Yeah, yeah." The boy unfurled from his slouch and slid down from the throne to approach Lucy and Dee.

"You may greet me, barbarians," the boy commanded them. He wore a long black silk robe with an embroidered blue-green dragon covering the front and a golden dragon on each shoulder. Four more dragons were embroidered around the hem of the robe.

But none of this grandeur can disguise the fact that he's a lot of boy, Lucy thought.

"I am His Holy Majesty, Emperor Yidi, and all that you see under the heavens belongs to me." The youth gave a grand, imperious gesture that set the long billowing sleeves of his robe swinging. He pushed them up, entangling his hands in the process. Extricating himself from the fabric, he thrust out a hand to Dee. His sleeves promptly fell again to cover it and the young emperor made a rude sound.

Lucy shoved her fist into her mouth to prevent her giggles from escaping. Dee coughed and pretended he had something stuck in his throat.

Emperor Yidi went through the whole performance again, and this time Lucy caught sight of a heavy ring. "You may kiss my ring," he said. "Quickly."

Dee gave a jerky little bow over the emperor's hand and brushed his lips over the top of the ring. He turned to Lucy. "Your turn."

Lucy bobbed a brief curtsy and, grasping the pudgy tips of the emperor's fingers in her own, lightly ran her lips over the ring.

"You, barbarians, will come with me," the emperor instructed them before snapping his fingers at a guard. The guard turned and gave a low whistle. Four servants bearing a litter on their shoulders came running from the back of the chamber. They kept their heads down and their gaze firmly on the floor as they came to a stop in front of Yidi. Then as one, they dropped to their knees and one of the men behind the throne helped the young emperor into the litter.

The servants ground their teeth as the litter swayed and dug into their shoulders as Yidi shifted around to get comfortable. The servants rose to their feet and Yidi poked his head out of the curtains of the litter. "Follow me."

He shouted a command before letting the heavy curtains fall shut again. Two guards wearing red and black headdresses and armbands with a black griffin motif came forward. They carried polished axes and wore swords at their waists, and they fell in at the front of the little procession. Another pair of guards, also bristling with weaponry, fell in at the back. One of the front guards whistled and the servants moved off at a brisk trot.

"Wait," Dee cried. "We have to wait for the Xami."

"Too late," Yidi said in a singsong voice.

Lucy turned to look and then drew in a sharp breath.

With a shimmer of light and a glitter of scales, the Xami disappeared.

"Oh no," Dee said.

"They don't stay, you know," the queen's voice rang out.

Lucy shifted her gaze to the woman on the platform.

The queen seemed to attempt a smirk, but it was more a baring of her teeth. "So, you are here with us now. For better ... or worse."

With that, the queen rose from her throne, stepped down from the platform in a swirl of silken robes, and strode off through the crowd while calling for her attendants to bring her paper, brushes, and ink. Sabu stood, stretched, and sauntered after her. His paws, the size of dinner plates, made no sound. The portly man followed.

Lucy scuttled to the doorway where Dee stood shifting his weight from one foot to the other.

"How could you do that, Lucy!" Dee hissed.

"Do what?" Lucy had a niggling feeling she knew exactly what.

"Tell the queen everything. Do you think she's going to use that information for our good?"

Lucy, now deeply suspicious she had made a dreadful mistake, felt all hot and prickly. That was probably why she immediately snapped Dee's head off. "If it was up to you, we'd still be living a boring life!"

"I wasn't bored!" Dee sounded anguished.

Lucy chewed her lower lip and gave a short decisive nod. "We can't go back, so we must go forward." She pointed at the retreating litter bearing the emperor. "We might as well follow him. At least now we're having an adventure."

CHAPTER TEN

It seemed to take a long time to get to the emperor's destination, and the hallways had so many twists and turns that Lucy was soon hopelessly disoriented.

As they turned yet another corner, it was clear they were entering the quarters of the senior members of the palace. The hall was wider, and the walls were hung with large paintings and silk wall hangings. The floors made a deep, melodious twang under their footsteps.

"You'd think they'd get these creaky old floors fixed, wouldn't you?" Lucy puffed as she trotted along behind the litter.

Dee glanced at her but didn't slow his pace.

Eventually the servants stopped in front of a large set of double doors carved with dragons and birds. More guards in the red and black theme were positioned on either side. Lucy clamped her hand to her side to ease the cramp that had formed.

At another whistle from one of the guards, the doors swung open and the little procession entered another chamber. The guards fanned out along the walls as the servants gently set the litter down. A small plump woman in a simple gray robe rushed forward to help Yidi down.

As Yidi stepped out of the litter and dismissed the bearers, Lucy took the opportunity to look around. They were in a huge room lined on three walls with dark polished wood, the fourth wall was almost all windows with a door leading to a courtyard. Two walls were mostly covered with huge scrolls painted in delicate watercolors. On the third, a selection of swords and other blades hung. The hilts looked to be silver and thickly covered in gemstones. The blades all looked wickedly sharp.

A tremor ran through Lucy. She hoped there wouldn't be an occasion to use one of the deadly weapons.

She turned to look as Yidi walked toward her.

"Aren't you a complete idiot," the young emperor sneered.

"What!"

"Taking cakes from Xixi."

"I was hungry, and they looked good." Lucy protested.

Yidi shook his head. "Rookie mistake. She got you with a truth potion."

She shot Dee a look. *Well, that explains a lot.* Normally, she was much more cautious around adults she'd just met and not very talkative. And the queen had been so interested in her, not like her parents who only seemed to notice her when they wanted her to do something. "How was I to know? And who does that anyway? What a way to treat people," Lucy fumed. "Why would your mother do that?"

"My mother?" Yidi looked startled.

Lucy cocked her head. "Yes! Your mother, the queen."

"Oh, she's not my mother." Yidi snorted. "She's my father's second wife."

Yidi turned to talk to Dee.

Lucy chewed her bottom lip. She felt a little sick about telling the queen so much. She wondered what she would do with the information Lucy had given her. Trying to distract herself from thoughts of disaster, she wandered around the room continuing to examine its contents.

A square couch, draped in silks and covered in brightly colored pillows, sat in the middle of the polished floor. Scrolls tied with silk ribbons were piled high on a carved table.

"Who is this?" Lucy pointed to a partially unrolled scroll. At the top was a watercolor of a beautiful young woman in silk robes, and symbols marched in precise rows beneath the image.

"Oh, just some poet." Yidi sounded disgusted. "She's famous. My tutor wants me to learn all about her." He threw up his hands. "Poetry!"

Lucy moved on with her examination of the table. A mechanical clock sat beside the scrolls.

Various chests and other pieces of highly polished dark wood furniture were scattered around the room.

Two wooden tablets inscribed with rows and rows of writing were propped on a broad stone table that nestled in one corner. A small portrait was inset at the bottom of the tablet, a woman on the left and a man on the right. In front of them was a shallow dish filled with burnt bits of paper and beside that, a small green stone jar holding incense sticks.

"Who are these people?" Lucy called over to Yidi as she pointed at the photos.

"My parents," Yidi snapped. "Come away from there, it's private."

Lucy shrugged and drifted over to the wall composed of floor-to-ceiling windows. It looked out into a courtyard planted with flowers that she couldn't identify. Blue and yellow birds flitted between trees that ringed a central pond. A flash of glistening gold made Lucy gasp until she realized that it was only a huge fish jumping out of the water in pursuit of a bug.

Strangely the other three walls of the courtyard had no windows.

"We will eat now," Yidi addressed one of the servants who had melted into the background.

One gray-robed servant briefly rang a handbell. There was a hasty scurrying to set up a low table and three cushions on the floor. The door opened and more servants poured in carrying platters of food, which were then arranged on the table over braziers to keep the food warm. Lucy identified a bowl of rice, and on a platter, thin strips of meat were beautifully arranged in the shape of a chrysanthemum on a bed of greens.

"Duck, right?" Lucy said to Dee, tilting her head at the platter.

"Yep." He grinned.

Lucy beamed. Dee's Aunt Delia had served it for dinner one night with a delicious cherry sauce. She had always remembered it.

Platter after platter of food arrived. Lucy leaned forward to serve herself and Yidi held up a hand for her to stop. Startled, she sat back in her seat embarrassed she might have made a serious error in etiquette. She was probably supposed to let the emperor go first. Her own dinner table had been pretty much help yourself and don't take too long about it.

Once all the food was on the table, a different servant, holding a bowl, served himself a small portion of everything. He tasted it all. Yidi waited and waited. Lucy thought she was going to lose her mind the food smelled so good. About fifteen minutes later, Yidi nodded to the servant and leaned forward to begin to serve himself.

"Go ahead." He gestured to the food.

"What was that all about?" Dee questioned.

Yidi shot him an astonished look. "Food taster."

"Why do you need your food tasted?"

Yidi looked even more amazed. "To test for poison, of course."

"What!" Lucy pushed her bowl away.

"No, no, it's safe." Yidi waved a hand. "See, he's fine." He pointed to the servant who was just leaving the room.

Dee looked doubtful. "You suspect poison?"

"It happens," Yidi mumbled around a mouthful of food.

By the end of the meal, Lucy could feel her eyelids begin to droop.

"I'm tired now," Yidi declared. "In the morning, you will entertain me. I'm bored."

"How can you be bored being the emperor?" Lucy asked.

"Right now I don't like being the emperor very much." He chucked a pillow at one of the guards who allowed it to hit him. "I feel like a dress-up doll." He pulled his heavy silk robe away from his body and looked at it with disgust. "I am the Son of the Celestial King—the supreme ruler like my father, grandfather, and great grandfather, and all down the other greats." He pulled a dish of spiced fish toward him and speared a fillet. "And like them, I am the chosen one of the gods. It is my sacred right and duty to rule this empire. But I don't get to make any decisions. Xixi and her band of snaky sycophants do that for me. And they will continue to do so until I am sixteen. Three more long years." He plopped the fillet on his plate and cut into it savagely.

"*Three years!*" Dee exclaimed. He shot Lucy a meaningful look, but she ignored it.

Lucy focused on Yidi. *If it's his sacred right and duty to rule, then it's also his duty to care for his people*, she thought. *Not have them in chains.* She wondered how much he really knew about that. She decided to probe a bit.

She nodded with sympathy. "Grown-ups can be a pain, can't they? And they keep so many secrets."

Dee folded his arms and scowled.

"Oh, no one keeps secrets from me," Yidi objected. "I'm sure that I'm on top of the situation. I know everything that's going on in my country."

"You do?" Lucy raised her eyebrow. This kid was really something if he knew about the chain gangs and did nothing.

"So what will you do to entertain me tomorrow morning?" Yidi said.

"Entertain you?" Dee turned a perplexed face to Yidi.

Yidi waved a hand. "Yes, and you have to." He looked smug. "The Xami said you were here to be my companions. And don't forget, my word is law. If you don't obey, I can have you executed with one snap of my fingers."

Yidi held his hand up in the finger snapping gesture and Lucy pressed her lips together. *If this is how he treats his companions, no wonder the kid doesn't have any friends.*

Out of the corner of her eye, Lucy saw the guards stiffen to attention and grasp their axes more firmly. She gulped and slid her gaze to Dee. His normally pale face went whiter still.

"I'll think of something," Dee whispered.

"Go now." Yidi flicked his fingers at them. "I'm tired."

The sky had darkened, and Lucy realized just how tired she was. Dee must have felt the same because he asked, "Where do we sleep?"

Yidi rolled his eyes but clapped his hands. Servants materialized seemingly out of nowhere and led them to two rooms, which were side-by-side and just down the passage from Yidi's room.

Lucy looked in hers, it was simply but comfortably furnished, and the large couch heaped with pillows looked very inviting after last night spent outdoors.

"Dee, can we talk for a minute before you go to your room?" Lucy asked after the servants had left. "Do you think we should tell Yidi what our mission really is? That he's in danger and we're supposed to help him?"

Dee shook his head. "I don't think so."

"But testing for poisoned food?"

"Seems like a sensible safety precaution," Dee said. "I was reading a book about Egypt before we came here and the pharaohs had their food tasted all the time. No, I think we need to get to know him better first. He's not at all what I expected."

Lucy had to agree.

Dee said, "What's more important is that Yidi said he doesn't come of age for *three years*! How can we stay here for that long? Your parents, my aunt ..." His voice trailed off.

"You still want to find your parents, right?" Lucy said. "It seems to me this is our best shot at getting you the key to transmutation."

Dee nodded but he looked torn.

"We'd better hope time travels really differently here," Lucy said. "Although three days or three years, I'm still in a lot of trouble." Even knowing that, she wasn't ready to give up on her adventure yet.

After Dee left for his own room, she washed her hands and face using a bowl of scented water left on a stand and dried off with a thick linen towel. But as she crawled under the silk cover that had been folded at the end of the couch, she wondered again if she'd made a terrible mistake with the queen.

CHAPTER ELEVEN

he next morning, Lucy was awoken by a servant coming into the room and throwing back the shutters on the window. After a breakfast of flatbread and honey, she found Dee and they rejoined Yidi.

"Come here, barbarian girl." Yidi motioned imperiously for Lucy to approach him.

"Why do you keep calling us barbarians?" Lucy found the term insulting and didn't mind letting it show.

"Because you are barbarians!" Yidi looked surprised. "You are nothing like us. You have hair the color of gold, like Xixi's. And its twisted shapes look like egg noodles. You,"—he pointed at Dee— "have hair the color of flame and dark spots on pale skin." He stepped forward and touched one of Dee's freckles with the tip of his finger. "It's quite strange. But you're definitely not one of us."

"I don't see why it's strange, you've seen people like us before. You just said I had the same hair color as the queen. Mine is just curly," Lucy argued. "And she said that you had more barbarians here before—they just weren't children."

"No, the last ones were grown-ups," Yidi agreed. "Two of them, a man and a woman. They came oh, about four years ago. Yes, that's right because my mother was still alive, lucky for them. *They* didn't have the protection of the Xami, and Xixi would have had their heads on the floor, no questions asked."

"Why?" Dee was perplexed.

Yidi shrugged. "Because they were crazy. When one of our schol-ars finally figured out what they were trying to tell us, the barbarians said they were looking for a lost city. Really now, how can a city be lost! We all had a good laugh about that, I can tell you!" He held his sides, threw his head back, and let out a few hearty guffaws. "Yes, we laughed about it for days!"

Lucy felt the heat rise in her face and an angry retort spring to her lips. It was silenced when she caught sight of Dee. He had gone very still. "You okay?" She nudged him. "Oh ..." Understanding dawned. "Do you think they could be your parents?"

Dee slowly turned to look at her. "Could be," he whispered. "We found a way to Sericea. Why couldn't they?"

"What are you two whispering about," Yidi snapped, looking from one to the other.

"Nothing," Lucy said. "But what happened to those two barbar-ians?"

Yidi shrugged. "Don't know. Don't care."

At Lucy's fierce glare, he added, "But I think they continued on their journey. Still looking for their mythical lost city," he smirked. He looked at them closely. "You're hiding something. And I heard you say something about his parents." He pointed at Dee. "Where are your parents?"

"They are traveling," Dee muttered. "Doing important work."

"Without you?" Yidi's eyebrows rose. "What work is more im-portant than their heir?"

Dee just shrugged and Lucy saw his face crumple. She hoped Yidi wasn't going to pursue this line of questioning.

"Whatever," Yidi went on. "Enough about you. It's time for you to entertain me." He plopped himself down on the square couch and looked expectant.

When neither Dee nor Lucy moved, Yidi held up his hand, thumb and middle finger touching. "Just like this," he reminded them, an evil glint in his eye.

The guards tensed.

"Ooookay," said Lucy, thinking it was best to play along. "How do you like to be entertained?"

"Surprise me." Yidi said.

"Surprise you?" Dee couldn't keep a slight panic out of his voice.

"Yes." Yidi sounded impatient. "And make it good. I'm bored."

He turned to Dee who was pulling items out of the inside of his lab coat. "Now stop stalling."

"I will demonstrate that I can bring minerals to life and make them grow," Dee claimed.

Lucy looked at him in surprise. She wasn't particularly hot stuff when it came to science, but even she knew that minerals were lifeless and inert. At least where she and Dee came from.

"We will have to go out into the courtyard. We need lots of space. Some of the chemicals are dangerous to inhale." Dee said.

On the way out, Lucy managed to whisper to Dee, "Nightmare of a kid. No wonder Lord Petram said he didn't have any friends."

"What are you two whispering about?" Yidi called.

"Nothing," Dee replied. "Here, take Bertie while I do this, please." He handed over the little hedgehog and moved quickly away from Lucy who slipped Bertie into the generous pocket of her cargo shorts.

Dee hustled over to join Yidi.

Once outside, Dee opened his lab coat and took out a glass beaker. Into it, he dropped a lump of dark silvery minerals. "Hold this for a minute, please," he said to Yidi.

Yidi took the beaker and turned it around in his hands, examining it with a skeptical look.

Dee fished around in his pockets and drew out an indigo-blue bottle. As he pulled out the stopper he said, "Hold the beaker steady now, you don't want to get any of this liquid on you." Carefully, Dee poured the liquid over the silvery minerals. Finally, he pulled out a short length of coiled copper wire and dropped it in with the other ingredients. "There." He took the beaker from Yidi, put it on the ground, and stood back.

Yidi's eyes widened as small silver shoots grew out of the rock. A silver tree trunk formed and grew toward the blue dome of sky above them. The beaker finally burst as thick roots formed and thrust into the ground while the silver trunk and branches continued to shoot upward. Dee stepped back with an exclamation.

Lucy would have sworn that even he hadn't expected as powerful a reaction as this.

"Whoa! You don't see that every day!" Dee exclaimed. "How is this happening? Metal can't replicate like that to grow. At least not that I know of."

"Magic," Lucy asserted. "Definitely magic."

Dee shook his head. "Magic is just science we don't understand yet." He pulled his notebook and pencil out of his pocket and crouched to balance the notebook on his knee. There was the crisp rustle of a thick page being turned over. "Let's see, height about fifteen feet, width at the widest point of the canopy, about nine feet." He scribbled furiously. He looked up at Lucy. "If I find out enough about this place, it will all make sense . . . eventually."

Lucy heard the edge of desperation in his voice.

Yidi clapped his hands with delight as silver leaves unfurled above them and began to shimmer and wave in the breeze. "Wonderful!" He spent a moment untangling his hands from his sleeves as silver apples formed in the branches above them. One fell, landing at Yidi's feet with a metallic thump. Yidi scooped it up and clutched it to his chest. "Now, make me a gold tree and I shall be the richest emperor that ever lived!"

Dee shook his head. "No, I've performed one of the great alchemical experiments for you. That's it for today." He made a last brief note in his notebook, snapped it shut, and stuffed notebook and pencil back in his pocket.

"You *will* make me my gold tree, or I will have your head," screeched Yidi, brandishing his apple in the air. "You just have to try harder. I want to be the richest emperor to ever live."

"You don't understand," Dee said, still looking bewildered. "Believe me, if I could make a tree of gold, I would have done so long ago and never have had to come here. This has never happened before. Usually all I get is a beaker full of crystals that might, if you squint your eyes, look like a small tree. Nothing like this!"

He reached out to touch the tree trunk. "I don't understand," he muttered. "It's the texture of bark but definitely metal." He put his hands on his hips as he looked up into the tree.

Lucy reached up to finger a leaf. "It's soft, like a real leaf." A note of wonder crept into her voice. "It's so beautiful." A gentle breeze lifted the leaves, so they twisted and sparkled in the light.

"Dee, you said this is one of the great alchemical experiments," she said slowly.

Dee nodded.

"And turning lead into gold was another one." She pulled a silver apple from the tree and hefted it in the palm of her hand.

Dee nodded again as Yidi rushed over and snatched the apple from Lucy, who glared at him.

"Was what you just did a form of transmutation?" she asked Dee, as she walked around the tree as if examining it from all angles.

"Not really," he shook his head. "The process for creating this— what the early alchemists called Diana's Tree—was the precursor to finding the Philosopher's Stone, the true key to transmutation. There is no guarantee I could turn lead into gold here. Besides, I don't have the right lab equipment and I'm missing some of the chemicals."

"Enough excuses," Yidi snapped. "You will make me a tree of gold. Even if it takes the rest of your miserable life."

CHAPTER TWELVE

"But for now," Yidi continued. "You will pick all of the apples for me. I must hide them so no one else can take them."

Lucy watched him bustle back into his room and, after a brief tussle with his sleeves, hoick open his chest and draw out a robe. He returned to the courtyard and held the robe by the ends, fashioning a sling.

"Go on, climb the tree and throw them down," he instructed Dee.

"There has to be a better way," said Dee. "Do you have something I could use to hit the tree trunk? That might bring them down without me risking a broken arm."

"I don't care what you do, as long as you get every single one of them for me. They're mine and I don't have to give any to anyone else," Yidi said.

"Greedy little monster," Lucy whispered under her breath as she reentered Yidi's room. It wouldn't have hurt the kid to offer to share the apples. Even one apple could have made all the difference to Dee in his search for his parents.

Drawn by the pile of scrolls on the table inside, Lucy decided the boys could be left to strip the tree. There was a scroll with a beautifully rendered painting of the Xami on it that had particularly caught her attention. She cleared a space on the table and unrolled the scroll, frowning as it rolled back up as soon as she tried to read it. She used the mechanical clock to weigh down one end and both hands on the other before studying the thick brush strokes marching in regular vertical lines down the paper. The symbols were completely meaningless to her. She sighed. It seemed the translator worms only worked on spoken words. Even Lucy drew the line at putting worms in her eyes—if there even was such a thing as worms that translated the written word.

"Yidi," Lucy called.

The emperor turned from his supervision of the apple collection.

"Could you give me a moment's help with a scroll? It's important."

There was a pause as Yidi considered her request and then, feet dragging, he joined Lucy. Dee put down the makeshift sack holding the apples and followed him inside.

"This one," she pointed at the large scroll she had unrolled. "There's a picture of the Xami on it."

"So?" He shrugged as Dee peered at the illustration over Yidi's shoulder. "You got me back in here for that?"

"Have you read it? What do you know about the Xami?" The kind but mysterious creatures fascinated Lucy.

"That scroll is something boring that my tutor wants me to read, but I haven't gotten around to it yet." He started to leave. "I need to get these apples hidden before the witch queen finds out about them."

"Why do you call the queen a witch?" Dee asked.

Yidi rolled up the scroll and turned to answer him. "Xixi? Because she *is* a witch. No one knows where she came from, and she refuses to tell. She's certainly not one of us," Yidi huffed.

Not one of us, Lucy thought. *Perhaps the people call the queen evil just because she's foreign. That's straight prejudice.*

"She was so nice to me." Lucy said.

"But there was that truth potion," Dee reminded her.

"Yes, there was that." Lucy felt a cold shiver spread over her shoulders.

"One day, she, that tiger," Yidi shuddered, "and that wretched brother of hers just appeared out of nowhere, walked straight into the palace, and—"

"Was the man with the dead badger on his head her brother?" Lucy ran her fingers over the other scrolls.

81

Yidi looked startled at Lucy's question. "Dead badger? Oh, no, that's just bad hair. Yes, that was Wanset. Now, don't interrupt again. Where was I? Oh, yes—it was just after Xixi showed up that my mother died." He gulped, and for the first time, Lucy felt sorry for him. "And she bewitched my father. I don't see why nobody else sees it," Yidi continued. "Before the mourning period was even half over, my father married Xixi. Everything was fine for a few years and then he died too. That was"—he looked at the position of the sun—"one month, three days, and six hours ago. Now she's taken over. May she follow an elephant with explosive diarrhea!" he added under his breath.

"But a witch? Really?" Lucy began to think perhaps Yidi was exaggerating. She could see why he didn't like the woman. Lucy wasn't sure she'd take well to the queen either if she was in his shoes.

"Really?" Yidi's voice rose. "You doubt the word of the emperor?"

"I've been taught not to call people names. Certainly not without any proof," Lucy said.

"Right. Well, enough of this chitchat. I must hide the apples. This is the first time I've had any wealth of my own and I'm not letting Xixi have it. But what am I going to do with you?" He tapped his fingers on the table as he studied Lucy and Dee. "If I take you with me, you'll know where I've hidden them. If I don't, you'll go through all my things, and I can't have that."

"What kind of a joint is this anyway?" Lucy huffed. "I've never gone through someone else's things behind their back, and I've certainly never stolen anything in my life. Neither has Dee." She folded her arms tightly across her chest and scowled at Yidi.

Yidi hesitated a moment longer and then appeared to come to a decision. He turned around and walked toward the wall of his bedroom. At his touch, a door-shaped piece swung open revealing a narrow passage behind.

"Wow, a secret passage," Dee said.

"Not really," Yidi said. "The palace is full of these passages so that the lowliest of the servants can go about their business unseen. We have to take it because we have nightingale floors in our part of the palace. We can't get past Xixi's quarters without being heard."

"What are nightingale floors?" Lucy asked as she stepped forward to peer into the passage. It was clean and dimly lit.

"They're specially constructed floors that 'sing' out when someone is treading on them." Yidi turned slightly to reply. "That way no one can sneak up on us to do us harm."

Lucy remembered how the floors twanged like a guitar string on their way to Yidi's quarters.

"Follow me," Yidi instructed. "And keep quiet. The walls aren't that thick."

"We're going to have to split up the apples," Dee said. "This isn't a proper sack and they're too heavy for one of us to carry for any distance."

Yidi nodded and found an embroidered shoulder bag that he handed to Lucy and a small tablecloth that he used himself.

"Where are we going?" Dee whispered as he followed Yidi.

"To a secret room I discovered," Yidi said. "The older part of this palace has masses of rooms that are unused. I store all my special stuff there."

Prickles ran up and down Lucy's spine as the three traveled the twisting passage. The sensation increased when they heard voices. Yidi put a finger to his lips and motioned them to stop beside a small door. To the right of the door, at about eye level, was a narrow sliding panel. "It's so the servants don't enter the room and disturb something private," Yidi said, barely above a whisper. "Listen."

He carefully slid it across, giving them a limited view of the room beyond.

The chamber went up all the way to the roof and it looked at least three stories high. Daylight streamed through an open circle in the middle of a midnight-blue cupola painted with stars and planets. On Lucy's left, the most extraordinary bookcases she had ever seen stretched all the way to the roof. A series of ladders crisscrossed them so that every single book was accessible. And what books! There were more books than she had ever seen in one place. There must have been thousands and thousands of volumes: tiny ones, dumpy ones, some simply huge, and others so old and fragile-looking that the slightest touch might turn them to dust. All of them were bound in leathers of brown, red, blue, and green.

"Come to your senses, Xixi. These children cannot stay," said a man's voice.

Lucy craned her neck to look over Yidi's shoulder to the right side of the room. The speaker was Xixi's brother. He held a sheaf of papers and was pacing on an intricately patterned carpet. Xixi sat in a dark wood chair carved with writhing snakes threading their way through grape vines. Sabu sprawled between them.

"Who knows what crimes they will commit? Send them back immediately. They can show the guards the way. The Xami have left them. We can get rid of them." The portly man raised his voice. "Guards!" The door to the chamber opened and half a dozen burly guards stepped into the room.

"Are you mad?" Queen Xixi hissed, waving the guards away again. "Do you really want to send them back so they can return with even more of the unfortunate barbarians? No. They are never leaving here. But they may also be our means to rid ourselves of that trouble-some Yidi. The entire situation just might work to my benefit. The key to transmutation could be in our hands! Imagine the advantage I would have with that. I'd have an endless supply of gold. Imagine the armies I could build!" She gripped his forearm. He winced. With a fierce expression the queen continued, "And what is my gain, is your gain. Never forget that."

Releasing Wanset, who rubbed his arm, she drummed her fingers on the arm of her chair. "But now down to the business of today. Give me that list of names you have."

She ran her finger down the names and then pointed. "This one, this one, and this one. They are to be arrested and brought to me for sentencing. Execution will follow swiftly. I will not tolerate rebellious nobles."

"There is also significant unrest in Midlein province. I have heard of deputations being formed to petition you for tribute relief," Wanset said. "They say the laws are too severe, the taxes too high. They are not happy with your regency. They feel it's too harsh and they are wondering why the emperor doesn't intervene. There may be more rebellion growing there."

"Not for long. Any deputations that arrive here will never return home. Now leave. I need to think."

After her brother left the room, Xixi turned to Sabu. "Sabu, we need to talk."

The tiger gave her a look and strolled behind a tall screen of carved wood panels at the far end of the room. There was a soft swish of air and a faint yowl.

Lucy's jaw dropped as Sabu, now the largest man she had ever seen, walked out from behind the screen adjusting the folds of a long silk robe.

Sabu had bronze skin and the topaz eyes of a predator. He raked long tawny hair back from his face with one hand.

"Wow," breathed Dee. "What just happened there?" He craned his neck. "I wish I could see behind the screen."

"Yes, my lady?" Sabu's voice was a purr.

"What do you think?" Xixi inclined her head toward Sabu.

"The arrival of these foreign children has complicated things, and now there is the threat of more rebellion." He paused. "This could work to your advantage. If those peasants in Midlein province are already feeling rebellious and they want the emperor to intervene well ... why not give them the emperor?"

"You mean send Yidi, those children, and a few guards to put down the unrest?"

Sabu just smiled baring long white fangs. "A peasant army, sufficiently enraged, could tear them to pieces." He paced for a moment, deep in thought. "But let's not leave anything to chance. We will send some agents to the province to stir up more trouble and provide the local people with better weapons."

"Treason!" Yidi hissed. His face reddened as he stiffened, and his hands clenched into fists.

"Tear us apart?" Lucy said faintly. Her mouth went dry.

Xixi stood up and clapped her hands. "Right. I need to call our helpful friends. We need to deal with the threats without alerting Yidi and the barbarian children," Xixi said. She extended an arm, hand outstretched as if to grasp an object. A thick book with a red leather cover flew out of the bookcase, arced across the room, and settled gently in the queen's hand.

"Whoa," Lucy breathed. "Dee, did you see that?"

Dee's mouth opened but nothing came out.

"Please set up the usual room," the queen continued. "This will take a lot of energy so I will need two of them."

Two what? Lucy wondered.

The queen opened the book on her lap and started flipping pages until she found the one she wanted. She gave a satisfied sigh as she put her finger between the pages before looking up at Sabu. "Still here?" she inquired, sweetly.

Sabu nodded and opened the door. Xixi stood and, still holding the book, followed him, saying, "Once we are done here, we will give those children a new mission." She laughed.

It wasn't a nice laugh.

"Treason!" Yidi motioned them to hurry after him, and minutes later, they tumbled into a dusty room that was shuttered against the sun. He put his sack of apples down and began to pace as he raged. "The person of the emperor is sacred. No one dares to plot against it. I'll have her crushed under a steel door in the courtyard for all to see. I'll have her buried alive in the desert for the wild animals to find." He shook his fist. "I'll have her burned alive!"

Lucy took a step back. The look on Yidi's face terrified her.

Dee, ever practical, said, "How? You've told us she holds all the power."

Yidi snarled. "Unjustly."

"Yes, okay," said Dee. Lucy stepped closer to him. "But let's stick to facts here. What are we going to do really?"

"She's going to have us torn apart," Lucy quavered.

"Lucy's right," Dee said. "We have to focus on that right now. Do you feel ready to put down a rebellion?"

Yidi looked like he wanted to say yes, but reluctantly shook his head. "We have to come up with a plan."

"And I think it should involve getting away from the queen," Dee added.

Yidi nodded. "She wants me dead." His voice faltered.

"She wants all of us dead," Dee pointed out. "We're in this together."

Yidi quivered for a moment and then the color in his face returned to a more normal hue. He gave a brief nod. "Right, right." He stopped to pick up his makeshift sack of silver apples scooping two errant ones back into its depths.

"Right," Yidi took a deep breath. "Safety first, vengeance later. But make no mistake, the witch will pay."

"There is definitely something strange going on," Lucy said. "I won't doubt you again when you say she's a witch. I mean, what just happened there? First a tiger, then a man. And a flying book ... magic, for sure."

"The man could have been behind the screen all along," Dee said reasonably.

"Do you really believe that there was an elaborate hoax. A man waiting patiently behind a screen?" Yidi asked as he showed them a chest to store the apples in so they'd be secure.

"No," Dee admitted.

"How do you know about the secret rooms?" Lucy stooped to corral a silver apple that had rolled away from the rest.

"I had a friend once. He was the son of the head cook. He showed them to me." Yidi snatched the apple from her hand.

"What happened to him?" Lucy asked.

"Xixi discovered we were friends. He disappeared."

Lucy fell silent. *Maybe that's why Yidi doesn't have any friends. And now Xixi's planning to have me and Dee disappear too.* Her heart gave an erratic thump.

"That's done then." Yidi carefully checked the lock on the chest and led them back along the passage. All the while he muttered to himself about what to do, how to do it. "She. Will. Pay!" He stomped on his way, then burst out again, "Burn her alive!" as he hustled Lucy and Dee back to his quarters.

"Man the door," Yidi instructed his guards. "Let no one pass without my approval."

As the guards filed out, Yidi turned to Lucy and Dee and added, "That will buy us a bit of time if we need it. At least there are still a few guards loyal to me."

"I think," said Dee, "we got a little more than we expected with that expedition."

"Thank you for stating the obvious," Yidi snarked. He paused. "Gods below," he breathed. "The key to transmutation and Xixi? It would be incredibly dangerous for someone as dark and power hungry as her to have unlimited wealth. Armies would be just the start." He shuddered.

Lucy caught sight of the scroll with the Xami on it. "Yidi, could you read this now? I'd like to know why the Xami are so important. Knowing that might help us decide what to do next."

Yidi's fingers shook as he took the scroll from Lucy's hands. His lips moved a bit as he scanned it, at first disinterested and then with increasing excitement.

"Well?" Lucy tapped her foot.

Yidi slowly lowered the scroll and met Lucy's impatient stare. "It says here that seeing the Xami is a good omen. That's good news for my reign, I must say."

Yidi looked thoughtful as he ran his fingers down the brush-strokes on the scroll. "Aha! It says here that the Xami only appear when great changes are coming." He paused. "I'll bet it means I'm ready to take control now! Not wait until I'm sixteen. This is good news for me."

He continued to study the scroll.

"But it does make things more desperate for her," Yidi continued. "There are courtiers who will realize what the coming of the Xami means, and they might not be content to let Xixi run things anymore. And she will try to keep control at all costs. She wants the power all for herself. There is never enough of anything—land, property, money—for that witch. She wants it all."

"But if she doesn't want to give up control, it's all the more reason for her to find a way to remove you," Dee pointed out. "That's why she's going to send you—all of us—into a dangerous situation. We need to focus on that. We really do!"

"You're right." Yidi's round cheeks shook with exertion as he started to pace around the room.

"I really can't understand why they hate us so much. What have we done? We're just here to help you stay safe … oh!" Lucy stopped.

"Exactly," Dee said. "Yidi is in her way. And so is anyone who helps him."

"Wait, you're here to help me stay safe?" Yidi looked at them in astonishment. "Just you?"

Lucy nodded. "Until you can take the throne … and it had better not take three years."

"I'm doomed!" Yidi threw up his hands and looked around wildly. "We need to escape. You heard her. After she finishes whatever hocus pocus she's up to now, she's coming to get us."

CHAPTER THIRTEEN

"**B**ut"—Lucy bit her lip—"we rode in on the Xami; obviously, we won't be riding out on them again. And if we're on foot, it wouldn't take long for someone on horseback to catch up with us."

"Yes, I see what you mean." Yidi paused, his brow furrowed with thought. Then his face brightened. "I know! Camels."

"Camels?" Dee felt like he might faint.

"Sure, it's unexpected, so no one will look for us on camels, and it's something that kids do. I mean, they use child jockeys all the time for the big races. How hard can it be?" Yidi shrugged. "Besides, it's something that Xixi would *never* let me do. It's not the sort of thing the supreme ruler does apparently. I'd do it just to spite her."

"I've n-never ridden a camel," Dee's voice shook.

Lucy put a hand on his arm. "Come on, Dee. You'd never ridden a Xamu either and you were fine."

"They helped us stay on, I know they did," Dee argued.

"We don't really have a choice, do we? And you could always look at it as a new adventure. Don't you want to do that?"

"No, I do not." Dee folded his arms over his chest.

"Too bad. Your other option might be waking up dead," Yidi said. "We have to get a move on. You heard the witch."

Lucy rolled her eyes. "You're not being helpful."

"Okay," Dee sighed. "We agree that right now our lives are in danger and it's time to make a run for it, but I think we need to discuss our route."

"We need to head straight for the Silk Road," Yidi said promptly. "I heard you tell Xixi the way. Once I'm there, I can seek asylum from your leader."

"Not a good idea," Dee objected. "I think that'll be the first route the queen will take to look for us. Besides, what's to stop her and her guards from following us into the tunnel and into our world?"

He shared a look with Lucy. He knew that she wasn't keen on the idea of taking Yidi home and trying to explain him to their families either. Besides, it wouldn't be at all what Yidi expected. But they had no idea where they would be safe in Sericea. Going home seemed like the only option, but it would be easier to consider if Yidi was less obnoxious.

"We could ask Lord Petram to disguise the entrance after we're through," Lucy suggested.

"That might work. But I still think we need to take a more indirect route," Dee insisted. "Make the queen doubt the Silk Road is our destination." He turned to Yidi. "Do you have any maps in your pile of scrolls?"

After some searching and more bickering, they found some maps.

"If we take a barge down the river to here"—Dee illustrated by drawing a finger along a line on the map—"we can pick up what looks like a road here and make our way back to the Imperial Way where it joins up with the Silk Road about here." His finger jabbed at a spot.

"We don't know what the terrain will be like, or whether or not we will be able to summon Lord Petram, so we'd better take some provisions," said Lucy. "If we have a few days' worth of food, that should be lots. Assuming our new route doesn't take us too far out of our way. Then Lord Petram can give us a good dinner at the entrance to the Silk Road," Lucy added.

"You!" Yidi pointed to a servant who had blended into the background. "Fetch me a bag of—let's see—breads, pickled vegetables, eggs, spicy duck, and some fruit—nothing squashy or heavy—and nuts. Enough for the three of us. Oh, and cakes, lots of cakes. And be quick about it." The servant was almost at the door when Yidi added, "And three waterskins."

"It's getting dark now," Yidi squinted out the window. "We can leave soon."

"What happens when someone comes in?" Dee asked. "Servants have been in and out the entire time we've been here. Won't someone raise the alarm before we can get away?"

Yidi scowled and then his face cleared as he crossed to his table and plopped down in a chair. He pulled a large sheet of paper toward him, then grabbed a pitcher of water and poured a few drops onto a cake of black powder, producing a thick black ink. He dipped his brush into it and made firm strokes across the page.

The servant returned with the provisions, left them on the table and slipped silently from the room.

Lucy looked over Yidi's shoulder. "What does that say?"

"It says, 'Keep Out, Vital Experiment in Progress,'" Yidi replied, picking up the paper and waving it in the air to dry the ink.

When he reached the door, he flung it open and instructed the guard standing there to attach the notice. He slammed the door, and a few moments later, the children heard the banging of a sign being nailed to the door.

"There," said Yidi, with some satisfaction. "That should keep anyone from noticing that we're gone for long enough to give us a good head start." He crossed the room and flung open the lid of the carved chest at the end of his bed. After a bit of rummaging around, he pulled out a scabbard that he wrapped around his middle. He walked to the doors leading to the inner courtyard and, on the way, took down the short sword hanging on the wall by the window. He sheathed it in his scabbard then walked toward the windows.

"Can't we have weapons too?" Lucy looked at the blades remaining on the wall.

"No, they're mine," snapped Yidi.

"Seriously, what a greedy little monster," Lucy muttered under her breath.

Dee murmured agreement. "His attitude is going to make traveling with him annoying."

Yidi gave them a nasty look before continuing. "Here, take this." He handed Lucy the heavy silk bag that held the food. She adjusted the shoulder strap crossways so the bag rested on her hip.

"And you take this," he handed Dee another satchel, which held the waterskins.

They headed for the door again.

"Just a minute," Yidi turned and went to the corner of his room. He rummaged around for a minute and returned with a padded silk satchel slung over his shoulder. Then he stepped through the door leading to the courtyard. "We will escape this way."

Dee saw Lucy scan the solid walls making up the other three sides of the courtyard. "Oh, yeah? And how are we supposed to do that?"

"Wait and see, small barbarian," Yidi said with a cheerful grin.

The smile was wiped from his face when the guard stuck his head around the door to Yidi's room. Footsteps could be heard approaching in the distance. "She's coming, Exalted One," he warned. "Queen Xixi," he added in case there was any doubt as to whom he meant. "And she has her guards with her."

"Hold them off," Yidi pushed the door shut in the guard's face and slammed home the bolt. "Let's go." He beckoned to Lucy and Dee. "No time to waste."

He hustled across his room and out the courtyard door, around the silver tree and to the brick wall on the opposite side of the square.

After checking that Bertie was safe in his pocket, Dee slung his satchel over his shoulder and, motioning to Lucy to come along, followed Yidi.

Yidi ran his fingers along the brickwork of the wall until he let out a satisfied, "Aha." He pressed a brick and said, "The Emperor Fuxi commands." Cracks outlining a doorway appeared. "It really does exist," he whispered, his eyes bright.

The cracks slowly widened until the door swung fully open and revealed a staircase leading down. A gust of dry musty air rushed out of the blackness below.

"Wow," said Dee. "I would never have guessed that this was here."

"Well, that's the point, isn't it?" Yidi stared down the steps. "My father shared the secret of this passage with me shortly before he . . . died." Yidi seemed to choke on the word and there was a short pause before he continued. "But I've never actually seen it before now. Come on," he motioned impatiently.

"The outer wall is a false one to hide this passage," Yidi explained as Dee went ahead of him down the steps. "My grandfather had it built."

"Why would he do that?" Dee said.

"There have been a few rebellions. Some people have no respect for the divine right of the emperor to rule." Yidi shook his head. "Are you coming?" he called up to Lucy, who was hesitating at the top and gazing down into the inky depths.

Yidi pulled a candle from his pocket and almost dropped it as the sound of a door being battered down boomed across the courtyard.

"Get in here!" Yidi grabbed Lucy and yanked her into the passage, then slammed the door shut.

The darkness was absolute.

"Light the candle!" Lucy called out.

Yidi huffed and puffed, and Dee heard him rummaging in his pockets.

Silence.

"I can't. I forgot the matches."

"What!" Lucy sounded like she was about to give Yidi a big piece of her mind when she stopped. "Wait, there's something burning in my pocket!"

"Lucy, look!" Dee yelped.

Lucy looked down at the glow coming from her pocket. Gingerly, she reached in with her fingertips and withdrew the feather from Shuka. A prickly sensation raised the hair on her arms and her palms tingled. Light bloomed around the three kids.

"Let's go," Dee urged as the sound of footsteps approached the hidden door. Yidi hastily shot home the three iron bolts now visible in the feather's glow and moved down the staircase. "That will hold them for a few minutes if they figure out where the outside latch is. Now what is that?" Yidi pointed at Shuka's feather.

Lucy told him and he made a grab for it. "I want it," Yidi said.

"No, it's mine." Lucy clutched it protectively.

"I am the Exalted One. Everything under the heavens belongs to me!" Yidi made another lunge for it and snatched it out of her hands. Immediately, it flared into a searing flame. Yidi dropped it with a hoarse cry.

Lucy stooped to pick it up and it glowed softly in her hand.

It doesn't want you, Yidi, Dee thought.

"Keep your stupid feather." Yidi glowered at Lucy as he sucked on his singed fingers. "We don't have time to lose. Let's see if your feather will show us the way out."

Lucy held the feather aloft and its light bloomed in the passage. It was high and wide.

"Here, give me that." Lucy held her hand out and Yidi handed the candle over.

"Let's see if this works." She touched the feather to the wick of the candle and a flame sprang up. With a sigh of relief, Lucy trotted down the stairs behind Yidi, the bag bumping gently on her hip, while Dee brought up the rear.

"Where does this go?" Dee wondered.

"I'm not exactly sure," Yidi scowled. Clearly, he didn't like having to admit he didn't know something. "I told you I've never actually been down here. We will just have to find out for ourselves."

Dee's pocket squeaked.

Yidi narrowed his eyes. "What was that? It's not a rat, is it?"

"Oh, that's my dra—"

Lucy gave him a sharp kick to the ankle. "That's his pet hedge-hog," she said over Dee's protestations.

"Whatever. Just as long as it's not a rat." Yidi waved a shadowy hand but looked like he'd lost interest.

"Are you nuts," Lucy whispered to Dee, who was now hopping on one leg while he rubbed his ankle. "You saw what happened when he noticed my feather."

"Yeah, right. For a minute there I forgot who I was talking to," Dee said, now following Yidi.

The passage twisted and turned, then it narrowed.

"Can you go a little faster," Dee urged Yidi. "Someone could break down that door at any moment."

"Relax," Yidi called over his shoulder. "That door will hold off an army."

Dee gritted his teeth but held his tongue as he forged on ahead to pass Yidi. The young emperor might not be in a hurry, but Dee could hardly wait to get out of this passage.

The walls around them were covered in beautiful carved designs with gleaming olive and black stripes and golden diamonds. They shimmered and seemed to undulate in the flickering flame of the candle. Something about the designs made Dee's skin crawl. Sure, they were beautiful, but they were creepy too.

A weird rustling noise echoed down the passageway, and he picked up his pace.

It was a few minutes before Yidi spoke again, huffing with the exertion of trying to keep up the pace. "I must say, I am looking forward to seeing where you live. I've never had a real adventure. We just need stay one step ahead of Xixi," he said, speaking loudly over the strange swishing sound.

Something jabbed Dee in the back and he jumped. "What? Don't do that!" he snapped as he turned.

Yidi pointed and Dee's eyes widened in horror as his mind finally comprehended what he had been looking at all along.

The walls writhed as snakes slithered toward them. Their black eyes glinted in the light of the candle.

Lucy backed away.

"Give me the candle, Lucy," Dee ordered.

She looked surprised but handed it to him.

There was a plop as one snake dropped to the floor of the passage.

Then another plop and another as snake after snake dropped to the ground and surged toward the children in oily black ripples.

"Stand back," Dee shouted as he waved the candle at the snakes. "Maybe the flame will scare them."

The threat of fire seemed to slow them down, but it didn't stop them.

"Uh-oh," Lucy said, her voice wavering.

And then she pointed to the dead end.

ᴄHAPTER FOURTEEN

The white noise of panic flowed over her as Lucy frantically cast around for an escape. *There has to be some way out! Think! I have to think!*

"We have to drive the snakes further back. We need a bigger fire," Dee shouted. "Yidi, give me one of the scrolls you took."

Yidi opened his mouth to argue, looked at the snakes, and handed over a large scroll. Dee touched an edge to the candle flame and flung the burning mass into the advancing reptiles.

"There has to be some way to get out of here," Yidi said. "My grandfather wasn't stupid. Look around."

Dee ran his gaze along the walls. "Nothing here," he said.

Lucy looked up. "Wait, I think I see ..." She held the luminescent feather as high as she could stretch. "Yes, look!" Her voice rose with excitement. "There's a trapdoor. See, right there." She pointed. Dee and Yidi craned their necks and then agreed.

"That's great, Lucy, but how do we get up there?" Dee had his hands on his hips. "It's about fifteen feet up. We either need a long ladder or an elevator."

Yidi yelped as the sound of bricks shattering under the blows of an axe boomed down the passage.

"Yes, yes, I'm thinking." Dee scanned the area. "No ladder, no obvious doorway, and another weird carving on that wall ..." His voice trailed off as he looked up at the trapdoor again. His forehead creased.

"Can you hurry up? The fire's dying down and the door will give way soon," Yidi yelped. "Grandfather would have been sure to have an escape. Find it!"

"Hey, wait a minute. Look!" Lucy pointed at the carving on the wall. "I don't think that's another decoration or snake." She ran her fingers over a section of the wall. The shape was distinct under her fingers. "Nope." She peered at it more closely. "It's been painted to cleverly look like one but it's a—" She gave a little grunt and pried it from the wall. "It's a rope ladder and it's attached right beside a trap-door."

"I'll go first," Yidi rushed forward, pushing Dee out of his way, but Lucy was already halfway up the ladder.

"Let's see if you can catch me," she muttered. "Where do you think we're going to come out?" she asked, nearing the top. "I hope it's not under the soldier's barracks or something like that. We'd be done for."

There was a bolt and a thick iron ring on the trap door. The bolt slid easily. All she had to do then was give the ring a good pull and the door would be open.

Lucy gave it a good yank and the trapdoor stuck halfway.

A dense cloud of wet straw and animal droppings poured down covering Yidi, who was still waiting on the floor below, in spectacular filth.

Restraining a delighted laugh, Lucy gave the trapdoor another tug and it opened fully to reveal the astonished furry face of a long-nosed camel. "Looks like we're in the stables," she called down.

Yidi spluttered in indignation as he tried to pick straw out of his hair and clothes, but Dee grabbed the ladder and started climbing. "Get up the ladder," he urged Yidi. "It sounds like they're nearly done hacking their way through that door." Dee reached Lucy at the top as Yidi began to haul himself up.

Moonlight poured in the stable windows illuminating the puzzled face of the camel.

Lucy carefully eased herself over the edge. "There, there," she murmured to the beast. "Sorry we startled you. We're not here to hurt you."

Dee pulled himself up beside her, and they both watched Yidi's painful progress up the ladder.

"Doesn't get much exercise, does he?" Dee muttered.

Yidi uttered a terrified yelp, as footsteps thundered down the passage behind them accompanied by the shouts of guards. He almost fell from the ladder, which was now swaying dangerously against the wall.

"We're going to have to help him." Dee said.

"I suppose." Lucy reluctantly moved back toward the edge of the opening and, after putting the feather carefully back in her pocket, she lay on her stomach on the stable floor and reached her arms down to Yidi. "Take my hands, Yidi. Dee, grab my ankles and pull."

Yidi gripped Lucy's wrists. His death grip almost yanked her arms from their sockets as Dee got behind her. Holding her ankles firmly, Dee slowly dragged Lucy back across the stable floor as the camel stood back and watched with considerable interest. Finally, Yidi's head popped up over the edge and there was a fierce scramble to get him completely out, the rope ladder and trap door pulled up, and the bolt on their side secured.

"Whew, lucky it wasn't bolted on this side." Lucy wiped her hands on her shorts.

The sounds of muffled curses streamed up from below.

"We can still get away. The good news is the snakes will slow them down too. And it's going to take them a while to go back and around." Yidi huffed, his hands on his knees, as he tried to get his breath back.

Dee shook his head as he looked at the trapdoor. "The guards had axes, right?"

Yidi nodded.

"The trapdoor is wooden. If they find something to climb on, they could chop through the door so they don't have to go around. What can we use to make it hard to cut through?"

"We could put that over the trapdoor to weigh it down." Lucy pointed to a stone water trough she could see through the camel's legs. She stepped around the camel to the trough and gave it an experimental push. "It's going to take the three of us to move it," she added.

Yidi shook his head. "Not me. I don't do that sort of thing."

"Seriously, dude?" Lucy put her hands on her hips.

The sounds of heated discussion came from below along with some clanking.

Dee grabbed Yidi's shoulder. "Two words, Yidi. Midlein province."

"Right, right …" Yidi nodded and, somewhat reluctantly, positioned himself to push the trough with Lucy and Dee.

"Shhhhhh," Lucy hissed as the trough screeched across the stable floor. "This thing is going to wake the dead."

"As long as the dead don't include us," Yidi quipped. "Okay, that should make them think a bit," he said as they finished positioning the trough. "Let's go!"

They carefully pushed past the still bemused camel and opened the door to her stall. Dee shut it quietly behind them. Yidi muttered strange curses as he resumed picking camel filth off his hair and clothes.

Before them, Lucy saw a central corridor with box stalls on either side. Each box had a name plate above it. Fuzzy faces with protruding eyes and long droopy noses peered over the tops of the doors.

"Hey, you!" Yidi kicked at a young groom sleeping on a pallet near the door with his blanket clamped around his ears. The boy grunted, cursed, and then sleepily rolled over and cracked open a bleary eye. Then, his eyes widened, and he thrashed around trying to free himself from his bedclothes.

"Oh, my lord, Most Holy and High," he babbled, finally jumping to his feet. Remembering himself, he collapsed into a prostrate bow on the floor, his skinny buttocks trembling with terror.

"Get up." Yidi nudged the young man with his foot. "We haven't got time for this. We need camels and we need them now. Hop to it." He snapped his fingers and the groom struggled to his feet, staggering slightly. Lucy saw he was very young, hardly older than her, and very small and thin.

"Rouse another groom," Yidi commanded. "We will select our

camels while you pull your pitiful self together." He turned on his heel and, gesturing to Lucy and Dee to follow him, walked along the aisle between the stalls examining both the nameplates and the beasts. Lucy heard the groom shouting and answering cries from other grooms. The camels shifted uneasily in their stalls.

A tremendous bang sounded from the last box stall on the right and Yidi hurried toward it as several grooms converged on the same place. The door of the box stall quivered, and splinters flew in all directions. A loud chatter arose from the grooms as they tried to sooth the jet-black camel that thrashed around, furious at his captivity. The brass plate over his stall declared his name: Prince of Darkness. A crazed light gleamed in eyes that rolled wildly in Yidi's direction.

"I will take this one," Yidi decided. He turned to a groom. "Subdue him and tack him up. Now."

The groom took a deep breath and went to get the camel's saddle and bridle.

"Are you sure about this one, Yidi?" Lucy asked.

"This one is the only one for me. On this camel, I will enter your country as a formidable emperor, and all will know my power and might. Your leader will give me asylum as a great ruler, not some beggar."

Not likely, Lucy thought. *There must be another way to keep our promise to Lord Petram and get the key to transmutation.*

Lucy walked back along the row of box stalls to find a nice, quiet little camel. She heard another bang, a man's scream, and a stream of curses coming from Yidi. When she turned to look at the commotion, a soft nose poked her in the back, and she turned to meet the gentle blue gaze of a brown and white camel. "Look at how long and curly her eyelashes are!" she said to Dee, who had followed closely behind her.

Lucy looked at the nameplate on the stall. "Her name is Sparkle. And she does!"

Sparkle's coat was thick and fluffy, and she held her head proudly, appearing to smile as she looked down her nose at the children. Lucy reached up to bury her fingers in Sparkle's puffy coat, ignoring the faintly musty smell that wafted up between her fingers.

Dee picked a sturdy looking brown camel whose nameplate read Temujin. This one placidly chewed his cud and rested his chin contentedly on Dee's shoulder.

"Hey, do you want to know a fun fact about camels?" Dee said, stroking Temujin's large droopy nose. Not waiting for Lucy to reply, he went on, "Camels can sprint at up to sixty-five kilometers per hour and they can maintain a speed of up to forty kilometers per hour for up to an hour. That's pretty fast. ...." Dee looked at Temujin doubtfully and Lucy realized he had the same question she did: would it be fast enough to outrun the queen?

CHAPTER FIFTEEN

Yidi returned to Lucy and Dee with two grooms in tow.

"Saddle these two camels for us," he ordered the men before grabbing two padded vests from their pegs. "Here, put these on. And there's something else. ..." He conferred with one of the grooms. The man trotted off, returning moments later with two pairs of baggy pants, two pairs of boots, and a cloak for each of them. "You'll need these too. Change and be quick about it." Then he left for the stable yard to wait for them to change.

When Sparkle and Temujin were ready, and the bags of provisions firmly secured to their saddles, a groom led Prince of Darkness, more subdued now, to join them.

"Have you ever ridden a camel before, Gracious Lady?" The groom leading Sparkle addressed Lucy.

She shook her head.

The groom clicked his tongue and Sparkle folded her legs to lie on the ground. An ornate saddle sat atop a colorful woven blanket on her hump, and woven reins ran from a halter decorated with multi-colored tassels. "Fancy," Lucy muttered before turning to the groom, who gave her a few pointers on camel riding.

Lucy swung her leg over the saddle, settled onto the leather seat, and picked up the reins. The groom gave a strange double click with his tongue. Sparkle awkwardly heaved herself to her feet, almost unseating Lucy by rocking far back to get her front legs under her and then lurching forward to get her back legs up.

Lucy gasped when she saw how high from the ground she was, even on a smallish camel.

Once they had all mounted, the trio filed out of the stable yard, which was brilliantly lit by the rising full moon, and Yidi led them in a brisk trot toward the main gate. "The moon is a blessing and a curse," he muttered.

Lucy agreed. It gave them enough light to see their way, but it also meant the queen's guards could see them if they were fast enough. She didn't have much time to pursue those thoughts as she struggled to find the rhythm of the camel's peculiar gait, so different from that of the Xami. The closer they got to the gate, the harder Lucy's heart pounded. The fearsome guard creatures were just on the other side. She remembered the rippling muscles, the silvery white fangs, and the hostile gaze of the beasts. Without the Xami, would they be able to pass?

The night breeze brought the scent of the monsters to the camels, who then pranced and skittered. Lucy's hands shook as she tried to control Sparkle and urge her forward at the same time. She prayed that she wasn't urging them both forward into a dreadful death.

As they passed through the gates, the two lines of creatures turned to regard them with their burning red eyes. The largest ones sat by the entrance. The one on the right lifted his snout to catch their scent. He bared his teeth and a low growl rumbled up from the depths of his throat.

"Uh-oh." Lucy beckoned to Dee and, inclining her head to him, whispered, "Now what?"

Dee considered for a moment and then threw back his head and opened his mouth. Out poured the same notes the Xami had sung to give them safe passage on the way in.

The fire left the beast's eyes and he lay down, muzzle resting on his paws, signaling the others to do so too.

"Nice work," Lucy muttered to Dee as she urged Sparkle forward. "How did you do that?"

Dee shrugged. "Perfect pitch."

At Lucy's curious look, he continued, "I just hear musical notes once and I can reproduce them exactly."

"Amazing," Lucy breathed.

"It has come in handy for my cello practice," Dee admitted. "But what's really amazing is that the notes seem to be a sort of password."

"What are you two whispering about," Yidi snapped. "Let's get going."

The camels arched their hessian necks, and Prince of Darkness, pulling up now beside Lucy and Dee, went so far as to aim a gob of spit at their mounts before thrusting his head forward and breaking into the ungainly gallop typical of camels.

Yidi whooped, whether in surprise or enthusiasm, Lucy found it hard to tell, and the emperor and his camel shot down the broad avenue and into the silent town. The buildings were dark, except for a few cracks of light shining through upper windows where candles still burned. Prince of Darkness slowed, giving Lucy and Dee the chance to catch up. Lucy now had the chance to ask Yidi a question. "The courtyard has people and their carts and carriages in it all the time. Does everyone need to know the song to pass the Guardians?"

He shook his head. "Only strangers. The Guardians know the Sericeans." He led them through the rest of the town toward the main gate.

"It's locked," Lucy said as she spotted the heavy chain and padlock.

"They will open it for me." Yidi urged Prince of Darkness forward and, before either Lucy or Dee could stop him, he roused the guard in the gatehouse. "Open this gate at once."

"Who goes there?" The guard's voice was slurred with sleep.

"Your emperor," Yidi declared grandly. "And if you don't want to be executed for disobedience and sleeping on the job, you'd better hop to it."

"Good grief," moaned Dee. "Could he be any more obvious? The queen isn't going to have any trouble at all following us."

Yidi turned and glared at him before addressing the guard again. "Please ask my guards to attend to us in the Jade Forest as soon as they get their lazy hides out of bed. We will be seeking the Baize."

"The Baize, my lord?" The guard's eyes widened.

"Yes, and the queen will understand why. She will probably reward you for bringing her the information too," Yidi added.

The guard's eyes lit up with greed. "Very good, Most Holy Emperor," he said as he cranked open the gates.

Yidi immediately turned left, away from the direction of the river and motioned to Lucy and Dee to follow him up the hillside.

Lucy was so angry she couldn't speak until she finally burst out, "What are you thinking, Yidi, blaring our plans for the world to hear? Where are we going? And who, or what, is the Baize?"

"I'm not as stupid as you think. I was going over different strategies as we rode through town," Yidi snapped at her. "And every child in Sericea knows who the Baize is," he added loftily.

"Well, we don't, so you'd better tell us," Dee grumbled. Lucy knew he didn't like admitting ignorance about anything. "And why you'd tell the guard we are going to seek it."

"The Baize lives deep in the Jade Forest. It is all knowing and, like the Xami, can speak our language. Also, it predicts when powerful change that affects the emperor is coming." He shifted in his saddle. "If that dolt at the front gate tells Xixi we're looking for the Baize, it will make perfect sense to her. She will be angry she didn't think of it first, of course."

"What are you raving about?" Lucy snapped.

"Don't you see?" Yidi threw his hands up in the air. "She will think that we have figured out why the Xami came and are trying to confirm it by sighting the Baize. And according to our maps, the Jade Forest is in exactly the opposite direction to the one we plan to go. So she and her guards will hare off in that direction and give us some time to get a head start."

CHAPTER SIXTEEN

A few minutes later, Yidi looked back. Dee followed his gaze and saw they were now out of sight of the town gates.

"Right," Yidi wheeled Prince of Darkness around and took a path that wound around behind the town. "This is definitely taking the long way, but we will be able to get down to the docks undetected now."

Dee shifted into a slightly more comfortable position on Temujin's back as he looked ahead. *There's a flaw in our plan, I know it. But where?* He chewed his lower lip as he thought furiously. Twenty minutes later, the fishy smell of the river reached him, but by then he knew what they must do.

They came around the last corner and the docks spread out before them. Ships and watercraft, ghostly in the moonlight, bobbed gently on the sluggish current.

"Why isn't there a bridge?" Lucy wondered as she drew Sparkle to a halt. "That would make life so much easier."

"Because that'd be like laying down the welcome mat for rebels and invaders and saying, 'Come on in,'" Yidi snapped.

"Even castle moats have drawbridges," Lucy observed. "Which boat should we pinch?" She looked down the line of flat-bottomed boats.

"None of them," Dee said turning Temujin and urging him to the water's edge on the far side of the docks.

"None of them!" Lucy exclaimed. "How are we going to get across?"

"It's a fun fact that camels can swim," Dee replied, then he held up a hand and added hastily, "but no, not going to do that either, because I'm not sure how far they can swim carrying riders and we don't know what the currents are like. If we nick a boat here, someone's bound to report it in the morning and we're sure to be the prime suspects. Then Sabu, or some other tracking animal—dogs perhaps —will be able to pick up our trail right away. Follow me. Ride and talk."

The moon laid a bright path of light across the water making it easy for Lucy and Yidi to fall in line beside Dee as he urged Temujin into the shallows of the river. "Besides, I'm assuming none of us knows this river, where the rocks are and so on. It would be stupid to try to travel on it in the dark. So instead of doing that," Dee continued, "we're going to ride downstream until daylight, then we'll steal a boat."

"Why didn't we plan it this way in the first place?" Lucy wondered.

Dee shrugged. "We're basically following the same plan, steal a boat and go downstream until we can pick up a different road on the other side. We're just going to walk part of the way. I don't think any of us thought Xixi would be after us so quickly. It's almost like she knew what we were planning."

Yidi brought his hand down hard on Prince of Darkness's saddle. The camel shied with an indignant honk. "It's that new servant. The one who started a few weeks ago. I'll bet he's a spy for the witch." He muttered and fumed until Dee wanted to tell him to shut up.

They rode downstream for the rest of the night, every nerve straining to hear any signs of pursuit while keeping close enough to the shoreline so the camels could keep their footing. They were soon past the outer limits of the town. Gigantic black shapes rose on their landward side.

"What are those?" Lucy pointed at them.

"Cliffs. There's a valley between them," Yidi said. "That's where we bury our dead."

"Oh, a cemetery." Lucy nodded. "I'm glad our route doesn't take us in that direction."

Dee peered at the shapes. "Do you bury them in caves in the cliffs or in the valley?"

"Both," Yidi replied. "Emperors and their families are buried in the cliff caves in fancy tombs. My parents' tomb is the grandest of all." He puffed out his chest. "Lesser nobles are buried in the valley."

Dee nodded. This sounded familiar. "There's a place like this where we come from, in Egypt. It's called the Valley of the Kings. My parents went on a dig there."

"I'll bet they're not as magnificent as ours," Yidi said with satisfaction.

After that, the only sounds were the splashing of camels wading through the shallow water and the occasional cry of a night bird on the hunt. Once, Dee thought he heard a rustling in the bushes now lining the shoreline, but he concluded it was only an animal.

Light started to spread across the sky and Dee called the others to a halt. A small fishing village was ahead. There was no sign of a road leading down to the water on the opposite bank though. "Where are we, Yidi? I think we're far enough away now to risk taking a boat. We need to find a road on the opposite shore that will eventually get us to the Silk Road."

Yidi pulled a rolled-up map out of his satchel and attempted to smooth it out on Prince of Darkness's back. "We're here," he pointed to a small dot on the map. "We just need to get down to here." He jabbed a finger at a spot a little further down. "And we can pick up the road we decided on earlier."

They rode a little further until the village quay came into view. A variety of watercraft were moored beside the docks and some smaller ones had been pulled up on the stony beach. Small wooden houses were set a short way back from the beach.

Dee put a finger to his lips and whispered, "We're going to have to be very quiet. Sound travels well in the still air. Which boat are we going to take?"

"I hope the owner can find it after," Lucy worried. "This looks like a poor village."

Dee was already inspecting the available boats. "We need one that's close to the ferry barges they use near the palace. One with a wide flat bottom for the camels." He moved down the line of watercraft. "There! That one should do."

He pointed to a wide boat that was low to the water with a small canvas-covered shelter in the front.

With great difficulty they loaded the camels onto it. Sparkle and Temujin, initially suspicious, eventually knelt obediently, one before the other, in the middle of the boat and began to patiently chew their cuds. Prince of Darkness, mad eyes rolling, refused, planting all four feet firmly on the boat's deck. Foam gathered at the corners of his mouth.

"We'll have to tie his reins to the sides of the boat," Dee said. "We can't have him lurching from side to side or we'll capsize."

Dee started poling out into the river. It was harder than it looked, and he proceeded with caution. The river was broad and slow moving here but Dee hugged the shoreline. "This boat isn't built for rough weather," he observed. "Good thing it looks like a clear day." The sky was now shading rose and gold and a rim of the sun gleamed on the horizon. A flock of birds rose from the reeds near the bank at their approach, and drops of water fell like diamonds from their wings.

Yidi lounged under the canvas awning, their bags at his feet. Lucy stood beside Dee, watching for floating logs or barely submerged rocks.

On their way, they passed several fields. Groups of people already toiled under the strengthening sun. It promised to be a brutally hot day, and they had nothing to protect themselves.

Lucy walked to the front and stood beside Yidi.

"See anything odd?" she waved an arm at the field workers.

Yidi squinted. "No. Why?"

"Really?" Lucy frowned. "Look closer."

"Don't see why I should. They're just peasants," Yidi grumbled, but he shaded his eyes and peered again at the workers. Slowly he lowered his hand, a stunned expression on his face. "Those people are chained together! And two of them are courtiers who disappeared from the palace two months ago."

Lucy nodded. "The Xami told us those were people who had spoken out against the queen. She's enslaving anyone who disagrees with her."

Dee saw her give Yidi a meaningful look. He wondered how Yidi was going to get out of this one.

"After the disappearance of those two courtiers—and I never got a good explanation for that—I heard that their land and property became the property of the crown," Yidi said slowly. "In other words, she seized it. Doesn't seem to matter how much she has. It's never enough."

He drew back a bit when he saw Lucy's expression.

"Well what am I supposed to do about it?" Yidi snapped. "I asked for an explanation, and I was told it was nothing I had to worry about, that I should stick to my studies."

Lucy was still giving him a hard look. Dee was familiar with that look and was just glad he wasn't the recipient. It meant Lucy was coming to an emotional boil.

"What do you want me to say?" Yidi threw up his hands. "I'm in no position to do anything. And I didn't want to disappear too. And now we're on the run, in case you haven't noticed." Sarcasm dripped from his voice. "Slavery would be too good for us now. She'll only be happy if our heads are rolling around in the dirt." He turned to face Dee. "Pole faster," he shouted. "If we can see them, they can see us."

Lucy gave Yidi a disgusted look and returned to Dee's side. "What a jerk," she muttered.

"What he said sounded reasonable under the circumstances. It's clear he doesn't have any power," Dee murmured in return.

He thought it was a good time to distract her.

"Look, Lucy!" A trio of large gray torpedo-like creatures breached the water in graceful arcs beside them. "These look like river dolphins!"

Lucy laughed. "They look like they're smiling at us." Her face became serious. "Look out for the floating logs."

Dee turned his head. *Should I tell Lucy or not?*

The camels shifted nervously.

The decision was taken from him as one of the "logs" waddled up onto a sandbank.

"Oh! It's an alligator." Lucy said.

"I think it's a crocodile," Dee corrected her. "Look at its nose. Alligators have wide, shovel-like snouts. Crocodiles have longer, V-shaped noses. Look over there." Dee pointed away from the crocodile. "That looks like a black-necked crane."

"Can you pole faster?" Lucy said, still staring at the massive reptile.

Dee steered them well away from the crocodile. The river was quiet here and the current was taking them along at a steady pace. A breeze wafted the smell of tropical flowers over the water. Unfortunately they didn't quite mask the smell of the river.

Lucy curled up on a pile of sacks and fell asleep, her mouth slightly open.

Resting the pole against the side but keeping an eye on his surroundings, Dee fished his notebook and pencil out of his pocket.

"What are you doing?" Yidi asked, as he made his way up from the bow of the barge.

"Recording my observations," Dee said as he noted the river life they had seen so far.

"Why?" Yidi persisted.

Dee sighed. "It's what scientists do. My father always keeps a notebook with him to record and draw his careful observations on a dig." It helped Dee feel closer to his absent father when he used his own notebooks, like he was following in his footsteps and showing his father he could be just like him.

"So what's this important work they do? Work that's so important they leave you behind?"

Dee felt the familiar pit of emptiness open in his stomach, the one he never seemed to be able to fill. "They're archaeologists and before you ask, they've been gone for four years and yes I'm trying to find them. That's why we're helping you. If I get the key to transmutation, I will have enough money to do a proper search." Dee picked up his pole and stabbed it back into the water. "Now, are you satisfied?" he snapped.

Yidi drew his head back and his eyes widened slightly, but he gave a slight nod before he hunkered down beside Dee and pensively gazed out over the water.

A little while later, he said, "Where did your parents go four years ago?"

"They'd found a lost city and they were going back to do more research," Dee replied as he scanned the water for threats.

"How can a city be lost? That's ridiculous," Yidi snorted. "I mean, you can't just misplace a whole city."

Dee sighed. Clearly word usage was a problem here. "Cities can be lost if they fall into ruin through war, natural disaster, or some such thing and then people forget they existed. They can be covered with landslides or even other cities. The one my parents found disappeared about three thousand years before I was born."

"Uh-huh." Yidi looked at him skeptically. "And what did they find?"

Dee poled them around a shallowly submerged log before replying. "So far, some complete pottery vessels, some stone and metal tools, and what looked like the foundations of some large and elaborate buildings."

"Doesn't sound like much." Yidi snorted. "And that's why you're going through all this?" He swept his arm to encompass everything around them. "To find them?"

"Yes," said Dee.

"But four years, they could be—" Yidi started.

"No!" Dee felt the blood rush to his face and his hands tightened around the barge pole. "No, don't say it," he finished more quietly.

Yidi nodded. "Four years ... that's what you and Lucy were whispering about in my chambers. You think the barbarians who passed through here four years ago might be your parents!" Yidi's face lit up with the realization. "It's a cracked idea, but I can see how you got there."

He fell silent. Dee wished he would fall overboard.

"Still," Yidi said thoughtfully, "searching for your parents and their lost city—it will make a great cover story if we find we need one.

People will think we're stark raving mad but consider us harmless and inconsequential. Yes, good idea." He flashed a self-satisfied smile and wandered back to the bow to sit under the awning.

It was several hours later when Dee handed Lucy the map.

"The river's getting narrower and faster," Dee observed, his eyes scanning the water. The speed of the water here had cut deep banks on either side of the river. Heavy vegetation lined the tops of the banks. "How much farther until we reach that road?"

Lucy unrolled the map. "I'm not exactly sure where we are now, but it can't be too much farther. One or two bends at the most."

"Hope you're right," Dee said. He saw rocks appearing above the surface and the water between them became more turbulent as the river sloped down.

The camels became restive. Even Temujin and Sparkle had stopped chewing their cuds and moved uneasily in the bottom of the boat.

"Oh, whoa!" Lucy cried as white water tossed the boat from side to side.

Spray soaked them all.

Dee poled desperately to steer them away from the glistening black rocks.

The boat picked up speed. Dee saw Lucy crouch and grip the sides of the boat with both hands, her eyes tightly shut. She had a greenish tinge to her skin. Prince of Darkness squealed, pulling frantically on the reins binding him to the sides of the boat. Yidi was crouched in the bow with an arm over his head. The other hand clung tightly to the gunwale.

The boat accelerated and yawed alarmingly. Dee poled harder, struggling to steer well enough to keep them off the rocks. The prow came up and then smacked down, drenching them all with more spray. Prince of Darkness lashed out with a back leg, catching the pole Dee was using and splintering it. Now the black camel was within inches of crashing through the low side of the boat.

The camel's antics caused the boat to pitch steeply to the right and water poured over the side. Sparkle and Temujin struggled to get to their feet.

"Lucy, untie that camel. We have to get him off this boat!" Dee shouted. "If he kicks through the side, the boat will sink."

Lucy nodded and, pushing past the black camel, untied first one side of his bindings and then the other. The prow of the boat rose again. Prince of Darkness appeared to rear, then slipped, stumbled, and fell over the side of the boat, legs flailing to find a purchase that wasn't there.

Lucy raced to quiet Sparkle and Temujin, finally convincing them to settle back down in the bottom of the boat.

They left the floundering camel behind. Lucy ran to the back of the craft. "He's swimming," she shouted.

Dee looked back to see the camel reach the shallows and struggle to his feet. "He should be okay now. Let's hope we are too."

The black camel was now a speck in the distance. Dee let out a breath he hadn't realized he was holding. The camel hadn't been taken by a crocodile. There would have been no living with Lucy if it had. The boat seemed to be riding lower in the water and Dee looked down. Water came up to his calves. "Lucy, can you bail please?"

"Has Yidi got a piano tied to his backside?" she muttered as she grabbed a small bucket tied to a ring on the side of the boat and started scooping water out as fast as she could. It didn't take her too long to remove the water.

"You'd better sit down now, it's getting really rough," Dee warned.

The scenery sped past. Lucy and Dee sat in the bottom of the boat and held on for their lives. Yidi crouched under the canvas, his back to them. Dee thought he saw the road they meant to take flash by, but he was powerless to do anything but cling to the side of the boat. He had nothing left but his roiling thoughts.

This is so stupid. I'm never going to get home. I'm never going to be able to apologize to Aunt Delia for taking off without telling her where we were going. And I'm never going to find my parents. He couldn't tell if it was spray or tears that wet his cheeks now.

The water roared around them, foam soaking their clothes as the barge swept helplessly along in the current.

Beside Dee, Lucy shuddered, white-faced, as she adjusted her grip on the side of the barge.

The river eventually broadened into a placid marshy area, thick with tall reeds. A forest came right down to the shoreline except by a small muddy beach. They could hear birds in the reeds and the trees. Dragonflies pursued smaller bugs on the surface of the still water.

The boat slowed to a stop among the tufts of reeds. For a few minutes no one moved.

Then Lucy opened her eyes. "Thank heavens," her voice was a ragged whisper. "We made it. I can't wait to stand on solid ground again."

She looked expectantly at Dee, who shrugged.

"It doesn't look too deep here," he said. "We can probably wade to shore." He trembled after the terror of the last hour.

"Where are we?" Lucy wondered, gazing around.

Dee knew they were far off course. It had been ages since they'd shot past the road he'd meant for them to take. "Let's get this tub unloaded and then we'll figure it out."

CHAPTER SEVENTEEN

They struggled to get the remaining two camels off the boat, and eventually it capsized, tipping the beasts out into the shallow water. As she sloshed her way through the reeds, Lucy saw a flash of something out of the corner of her eye. For a second, she thought she'd seen the queen's face, but no, it had to be a trick of the setting sun. Lucy shrugged and continued to trudge the last few feet to the muddy beach.

By the time she got to shore, Dee and Yidi were poring over the map.

"It looks like we've ended up in the Marshes of Moreton. We're now about one hundred and fifty miles from the palace," said Dee.

"That should be safe enough. For now," Yidi muttered.

"We should see if we can find a road," Dee observed. "There's not a lot of detail on this map, though."

"Well someone decided to burn the good one," Yidi said.

"You're the one who handed it to me," Dee snapped.

Yidi sneered. "I suppose you'd have preferred a snake necklace."

"Oh, cut it out," Lucy said. "We needed to hold off the snakes in the passageway. It's unfortunate we destroyed the detailed map but probably not a train smash."

"A what?" Yidi looked bewildered.

"Oh, never mind," Lucy waved a dismissive hand. "Now, where do we go next?"

Dee peered at the map again. "I don't know if there are villages or roads nearby. Maybe we can get back on track."

"Let's have something to eat first," Lucy said. "I'm starved. We can have a little picnic here." She pointed to a grassy area under a tree. She held out her hand to Yidi. "I'll take the provisions bag and set us up."

Yidi shuffled his feet. Lucy was sure she saw his cheeks darken with a flush.

"What?" Lucy asked. "You have the bag, right?"

"I never carry things," Yidi said, his mouth set in a sullen line. "There are people to do that for me." He gave Lucy a sharp stare. "Why didn't you grab it? I see you managed to lose the bucket along the way," he added triumphantly.

Lucy was speechless. And then something snapped within her. All the terror pent up over their descent through the rapids flooded out as white-hot rage.

"What?" Lucy whirled on him, hands on her hips and eyes blazing. "Why should we do everything? We're all in this together. Don't you ever think of anyone but yourself?" Her voice rose to a shriek and a flock of startled birds whirred up from the surrounding trees.

Yidi drew himself up to his full height, which wasn't far. "You are not permitted to speak to me this way!" he shrieked. "With one snap of my fingers ..." He held his hand up in the by-now-familiar gesture.

"Yes?" Lucy radiated fury. "With one snap of your fingers ... what?" She gestured at the empty space around them.

Yidi deflated like yesterday's balloon as he realized that he had no guards, no one to do his every bidding, and that he had to stand on his own two feet for once—and face-to-face with a girl who was hopping mad at him. He took a step back.

"Yes, well I'm the one with the sword," he mumbled as he unsheathed it and brandished it in Lucy's direction. "And I'm not afraid to use it."

"Argh!" Lucy threw up her hands and screamed. Then burst into noisy sobs. She stomped off and threw her arms around Sparkle's neck, burying her face in the camel's fur.

"She's not wrong, you know," she heard Dee say as his footsteps came closer.

"Lucy, you okay?"

Lucy turned a tear-stained face to him. She drew the back of her hand across her face.

"Maybe we could call Lord Petram and he could provide some food for us."

Dee shook his head. "Look around, Lucy. There's no visible rock."

Lucy looked. Dee was right. There was just the muddy area around the marsh and leaf strewn earth under the trees and bushes. Lucy drew in a deep breath. She'd really and truly had enough now, and a full-throated scream was building up inside her.

"There seems to be a trail over there," Dee said hastily, pulling her gently away from Sparkle and pointing just to their right. "And look, there are plenty of berry bushes over there."

Dee was right, there was a cluster of berry bushes, each with a protective armor of thorns.

"Lucy!"

She whirled around to see Yidi holding something dripping aloft.

"It was floating in the reeds. The food is all gone, must have fallen out."

Lucy advanced on Yidi who clutched the soggy provisions bag to his chest. She snatched it from him and marched over to the berry bushes. Dee followed in her wake.

"I know the kid is in danger. And I know our mission is to protect him." Lucy angrily stripped plump blackberries from their branches stopping to suck her thumb when a thorn pierced it. "But right now, his greatest danger is me. I could strangle him." She drew a grimy hand across her forehead. "I'm beginning to think we should find a village, leave him there, and just go home."

"It's a possibility, our lives are in danger now. We didn't expect anything like this when we agreed to our mission," Dee said, carefully avoiding the thorns. "I wouldn't get the key to transmutation, but it's not all about me."

Lucy took a deep breath. She knew completing this mission was

Dee's best shot in his quest to find his parents. "No, we'll go on. I'll try harder. Maybe I can get through to Yidi."

They wandered back to where Yidi had plopped himself down on a fallen log.

Taking another breath and pasting a smile on her face, Lucy said, "We found some nice blackberries. Would you like some?" She held the bag out to Yidi.

He took it, looked inside, and then dropped it.

Lucy had come to recognize the signs. Yidi had a way of raising one eyebrow when he was about to say something offensive. "I'm not eating that muck," Yidi said dismissively.

"Of course you aren't," she snapped. "You're waiting for someone to conjure you up a three-course meal." She crammed a handful of berries into her mouth and headed for Sparkle.

"We should get ready to move on, Lucy," Dee called after her. "We have to find a place to sleep tonight."

Lucy and Dee approached their camels. Lucy jerked her head back at Yidi.

Yidi remained standing. "Oh, right," muttered Dee. He and Lucy looked at each other. Neither one wanted Yidi on their camel, but both realized they would go faster if he wasn't trailing behind on foot.

Lucy still radiated fury. Dee sighed. "Alright then, Yidi, come on up with me.

"You'll have to get out of the saddle. You can sit behind me and hang on to the back," Yidi demanded.

"Say what?" Dee's eyebrows rose in astonishment.

Yidi stamped his foot. "I am the Exalted One, Emperor of All the Lands under the Heavens. I will sit in the saddle."

"Exalted One," Lucy snorted. "Exalted pain in the backside is more like it," she added, but under her breath.

A few moments later Sparkle and Temujin rose from their kneeling positions and onto their broad flat feet. Temujin staggered and Yidi, perched triumphantly in the saddle, smacked him hard with the crop.

"Hey," Dee objected from his precarious perch on Temujin's

hump. "It's not the camel's fault that he's been asked to carry excess weight."

Yidi opened his mouth, but Lucy interrupted before he could carry the argument any further. "You guys had better save your breath, we probably have a long ride ahead of us."

The rest of the afternoon wore on, one monotonous camel step at a time.

Dusk fell, and a fingernail of moon peeked above the trees.

"We will have to stop for the night," Lucy said.

"Where are the lodgings?" Yidi looked around. "I see nothing."

"There are no lodgings, Yidi," Lucy sighed. "We'll have to sleep outside. We can wrap ourselves up in our cloaks and cuddle up to the camels for warmth. Sparkle doesn't mind, do you my beautiful fluff ball?" Lucy dug her fingers into Sparkle's thick coat.

"Sleep out here?" Yidi screeched, causing the camels to shy like startled mustangs.

"Oh, brother," muttered Dee. "Here we go again."

Lucy clicked her tongue as the young groom had taught her. She leaned back as Sparkle sank to her front knees before folding her back legs.

Temujin followed Dee's command and folded his front legs.

"Argh!" Dee shrieked as he slid backward, arms flailing, as Yidi leaned further back than was necessary and forced him off the back of Temujin. He landed on the trail with a thump.

Taking Sparkle's reins in her hand, Lucy turned to the boys. "That looks like a good clearing just over there."

CHAPTER EIGHTEEN

The narrow path forced them to walk single file with Sparkle in the middle and Temujin bringing up the rear. The woods thickened and the dense foliage became menacing. Dark clouds gathered, and an ominous gloom settled between the trees. The path opened into a small clearing.

"These will protect us from any bad weather and make us harder to see too," Lucy pointed to the thick canopy of branches that arched over the clearing.

"It's very dark in here," Yidi whined.

"Easier to sleep that way," said Lucy.

"This is going to be very uncomfortable," Yidi groused. "And I'm very hungry."

"You're just going to have to suck it up," Lucy snapped. "It's more important that the camels get grass and water. We have plenty of grass here for them"—she scuffed her foot through the thick tufts of grass blanketing the forest floor—"but we need to find them some water." She untied her waterskin from Sparkle's saddle. "And we will have to top up our waterskins too. You did bring your waterskin, Yidi, didn't you?"

He opened his cloak to show her he had it fastened around his waist.

"Well, at least there's that," she muttered.

In the meantime, Dee had made a circle of stones and collected some twigs and fallen branches. "Before you go stomping off, Lucy, do you think you could use your feather to light a fire so we don't all freeze to death tonight?"

"It should work. It worked on the candle in the escape tunnel," Lucy said.

Moments later a small campfire was blazing brightly in the middle of the clearing.

"Right, I'm off over there." She pointed to the other side of the clearing, then she walked along the bushes, listening intently. She stopped.

"Dee," Lucy called. "Can you come here? I think I hear a stream on the other side of these bushes."

"They're awfully thick," Dee said, looking doubtful. "Look at the size of those leaves!" He pointed to the massive, bowl-shaped leaves. "We could force our way through them, but the camels would have a tough time. There has to be a better way."

Lucy snapped her fingers. "There is." Lucy called, "Yidi, we need to borrow your sword."

"No." Yidi had flopped down onto the ground on the other side of the clearing, his arms crossed and his lower lip out.

"Oooookay," said Lucy under her breath as she walked over to the sulking boy. Her fingers twitched with a strong urge to give him a good smack, but while it might make her feel better momentarily, it was unlikely to get Yidi to cooperate.

She squatted down beside him and stretched her arm out to put her hand on his shoulder. Thinking better of it, she drew her hand back before she spoke. "Look, Yidi, I know you're tired. I get that. But we need to stay well ahead of the queen. You said so yourself. If the camels aren't fed and watered, they won't be able to travel as fast tomorrow."

Yidi shook his head. "I didn't say no because I didn't want to help," he explained. "It was because this sword"—he drew it from its scabbard—"is simply ceremonial. It has a blunt edge. See?" He ran his thumb over the edge of the blade and then showed it to Lucy. There wasn't a mark on it.

"Really?" Lucy fumed. "And you had the nerve to threaten me

with it? Give it to me!" she demanded. Yidi handed it to her. She turned the sword over and over in her hands so that the gems on the hilt flashed in the firelight. "It would be nice"—Lucy ran her thumb over the blade just to make sure Yidi wasn't trying to pull a fast one— "if this was actually useful. She handed the sword back to Yidi and sat down with a thump.

"What? You think Xixi would give me something to defend myself with? Don't be ridiculous. But if people don't know the sword is only ceremonial, it's still a useful threat. It still might come in handy," he argued. "And only important people have swords like this."

"Well, now what?" She cupped her chin in her hand and stared into the fire.

"Camels can go for ages without water," Yidi said, yawning.

"Up to six or seven months," Dee agreed. "Here's another fun fact about camels! They store the water they need in their humps, and they get a lot of it from grass and leaves."

"And how do you know so darn much about camels?" Lucy snapped at Dee as she scrambled to her feet to unsaddle Sparkle and let her nose around in the grass.

"I did a project on them at school last year," he replied.

"What about Bertie?" Lucy argued. The little hedgehog poked his snout out of Dee's pocket at the sound of his name. "He can't go for months without water."

"I gave him the last of my water a few miles ago. I think he'll make it until morning." Bertie blinked, seeming to agree. Dee put the hedgehog down and Bertie foraged for the creepy-crawly things, like ant and millipedes, that he loved to eat.

"Whatever." Lucy's jaw set in a stubborn line. She knew that Sparkle needed a drink and if these two lumps weren't going to help, well, she would just have to do it herself. Otherwise, she would worry all night.

The thick blanket of stars overhead gave enough light for Lucy to see, and she forced her way through the thick bushes. The bowl-shaped leaves gave her an idea, and after a struggle, she managed to twist one off.

On the other side of the bushes was the bank of a river. Lucy hoped it was a different river and they hadn't just gone in a big circle. She sat back on her heels for a minute. She'd ask Dee when she got back to pull the map out again.

Starlight sparkled on the surface of the water as she knelt to scoop the leaf in. A splash indicated the presence of a fish rising to the surface to catch a bug. The water rippled as currents eddied and swirled. It had a dank smell, and the bank was slick with rotting vegetation. Lucy held her breath.

The surface of the river fractured. Drops of foul-smelling water cascaded around Lucy as long slippery black shapes reared out of the water. Sharp teeth snapped at Lucy's arm, narrowly missing as she fell back onto the bank. She screamed, scrambling backward on hands and feet.

Hideous slithering sounds came from the riverbank and some-thing thick and cold wrapped itself around her ankle. Another snake wound itself around her other thigh and squeezed tightly. Lucy thought her throat would tear from her screaming as she frantically tried to push the slimy serpents off her legs.

A tail whipped around and smacked her across the face. Her head snapped back with a crunch.

She screamed again. This time it ended in a whimper.

Light flared. "I'm coming, Lucy!"

With a rustle and snap of breaking foliage, Dee crashed through the bushes, a blazing torch in his hand, and Lucy saw the true hid-eousness of the creatures surrounding her.

They were about three meters long and thick as a man's leg. Mottled brown skin shone with a sickly sheen in the torchlight, and eyeless heads—sightless, but with huge nostrils—sensed the danger of the fire. They rose and wove back and forth to determine the direc-tion of the threat.

A searing pain ripped up Lucy's leg and settled in a blinding white fog in her brain.

Dee raced toward them, brandishing his torch. "Get away," he screamed, thrusting the flames at first one monster and then another. Finally, he drove the last one back into the water.

"You okay?" He held out a hand to help Lucy up.

"I'll live." Her voice shook as she allowed Dee to help her to her feet. Another bolt of pain shot through her. "Snakes! Argh!!" she whispered.

"Not snakes." Dee shook his head. "River eels."

An unreasoning anger shook Lucy. "Do you have to be such a know-it-all?" she snapped.

"Sheesh, you'd think you'd be grateful for the help," Dee muttered behind her.

Lucy felt weakness overtake her and her head began to swim. She wavered and Dee only just managed to catch her as she collapsed.

"You're hurt." He brought his torch down so he could examine her left calf.

Blood flowed freely from two rows of punctures, each row about three inches long. Lucy felt faint. She had never been comfortable around the sight of blood. Especially her own. She turned her face away and took a deep, shuddering breath.

"Ewww," said Yidi, who had just come on the scene.

"It doesn't look good," Dee admitted, examining the deep punctures in Lucy's leg. "One of the eels must have bitten her." He rocked back on his heels. "She's bleeding heavily, and those wounds need disinfecting."

He stood and looked down at Lucy. "Is your waterskin empty?"

Lucy shook her head and whimpered as a fresh bolt of agony tore up her leg.

"I'll be right back. I promise," Dee said. "Watch her," he instructed Yidi.

Lucy heard him crash back through the foliage, and he returned a few minutes later with two waterskins. "You and Lucy haven't finished yours yet," he said to Yidi. "I'm sorry but we're going to have to use what's left in both waterskins to clean the wound. The river water is too foul, and we don't have a container to boil it in."

"Wait! What?" protested Yidi. "I didn't agree to that."

"Not negotiable," Dee said through gritted teeth.

"Could we just get on with it?" Lucy moaned. "This hurts like nobody's business." She really, really hoped Dee knew what he was doing. She dug her fingernails into her palms as a fresh wave of agony coursed up her leg.

Shedding his riding vest, Dee pulled off his lab coat. He laid it out flat on the grass and ran his fingers over the bottles hanging within. "This one should do." He pulled a dark bottle out of its loop and set it down beside him.

"Yidi, can you hold her leg still while I pour water into the bite to wash it out?" Dee twisted the cork out of the first waterskin.

"Gross," Yidi muttered, but he squatted down to hold Lucy's leg still. He wasn't gentle and Lucy whimpered as her leg throbbed even harder.

"And now for some antiseptic soap to clean the edge of the wound." Dee unscrewed the top of the dark bottle. "Keep holding her down, Yidi, I hope this doesn't sting too much ..." Dee's voice trailed off as he poured the clear solution around the punctures.

Lucy writhed but bit back a scream.

The solution pinkened with blood. Dee waited a moment then ripped an arm from his lab coat. "I'll have to bandage it tightly to stop the bleeding," he said as he tore off a piece to wipe the blood and antiseptic soap away. "Boy scout training," he said in response to Lucy's questioning eyes. "And Aunt Delia helped me learn first aid."

He deftly tied the remainder of the sleeve around her calf.

"That's the best we can do for now," Dee said, rocking back on his heels.

Between the two of them, Dee and Yidi managed to get Lucy to her feet. She took a careful step and then another until she gave them a short nod. Her leg hurt like blazes, but she thought she could make it on her own.

"Thanks." She winced and started a halting walk again, weaving slightly but heading straight for Sparkle.

"Shush, shush," she instructed her camel. Sparkle lifted her head from the grass she was cropping and obediently sank down on her knees. Lucy dropped to the ground and threw her arms around the camel's neck and buried her face in the thick fur. "That. Was. Awful," she whispered. The wound in her leg throbbed in time with her words.

Lucy took a deep breath and wrapped her cloak around her before she cuddled up to Sparkle. "You know, Sparkle," she confided to the camel. "Adventures aren't all fun and games. They can be painful and dangerous and frightening." A sob caught at the back of her throat, "and I didn't even get you a drink of water!"

As she was finally dozing off, Lucy heard movement around the little clearing as Yidi and Dee followed her lead. Her eyelids grew heavy and before long, she fell into a restless sleep, lulled by the strong beating of Sparkle's heart.

CHAPTER NINETEEN

The next morning dawned bright and clear. Songbirds warbled above Lucy as she stretched and stood to ease muscles cramped from a night on the hard ground. Fire seemed to rip up her leg. She looked down. Her bandage had unraveled, and the eel bite looked swollen and red. Two thin red lines had begun to creep up her leg. *That can't be good.* She made a face and then gingerly took the ends of the torn sleeve and bound it up again. *Riding isn't going to be terribly comfortable today.* She sighed as she eased down the leg of her riding pants. Tears filled her eyes as she struggled to put her boot on over her hurt leg.

"Come on sleepyheads." She nudged Dee and then Yidi with the toe of her other boot. "We'd better get going." She looked at the vivid blue sky. "Today's sure to be a better day. What could go wrong?" Her boundless self-confidence couldn't stay squashed for long.

"Xixi could catch us," Yidi, always a killjoy, pointed out as the two boys stumbled sleepily to their feet.

"So far, we haven't seen any sign of the queen or her troops, so we must be well ahead," Lucy insisted.

Just then there was a loud thwock beside her right ear. Slowly she turned to see an arrow quivering in the tree beside her. It was quickly followed by two more.

Through the trees, Lucy saw half a dozen boats lined up on the river facing the shore. About two dozen archers wearing the blue and gold of the queen stood in the bows as the oarsmen brought them closer to shore.

"Run!" Dee cried. "And stay low."

"What about Sparkle and Temujin?" Lucy asked.

Yidi picked up the satchel that he had used as a pillow and slung it across his neck.

"We can't get them saddled in time, and we're less of a target without them," Dee shouted as he ran.

"They'll be fine." Yidi panted as he hustled through the forest. "A couple of the archers will be happy to take them back and collect the reward. Keep running."

"We don't know where we're going," Lucy pointed out, but she kept dodging from tree to tree, moving forward as fast as she could. Another arrow struck a tree just to her left.

"The important thing right now," Dee said, "is not where we're running to, but what we're running from. And right now, we have two advantages." He panted. "They still have to disembark, and they can't get an accurate shot with all the trees and bushes in the way."

Lucy heard the archers crashing through the underbrush some ways behind them.

The trees thinned and they stumbled onto a road. The other side of the road dropped off steeply into a valley far below.

"What are we going to do now?" Lucy wailed. Her injured leg felt like someone was driving hot knives into her calf. "If we stay in this forest, they'll catch us, but if we run along the road, they'll have a clear shot at us."

Dee made a sharp turn and began to run along the road, dodging every so often into the bushes. "Keep up!" He waved his arm at them.

Lucy looked back. The archers were gaining. She began to run again, but every step set off flashes of agony.

Dee and Yidi were well ahead of her now. She tried to run again, and again had to hobble to a halt. She couldn't run any further. Now she was going to get them all captured ... or worse. Tears and a scream of frustration threatened to burst out.

Dee looked back and slowed down. "Lucy! Come on!"

"I can't, Dee," Lucy sobbed, bent over with her hands on her knees. "I can't run anymore." She straightened up, tears running down her cheeks. "Go on, you and Yidi run. I can slow them down a bit. Maybe they just want to capture us."

Dee shook his head as he ran back toward her. "Not happening. We'll find another way."

Yidi pointed to the rapidly approaching archers. "We need to keep running! They aren't in range to get a good shot yet. But they will be soon." He set off again at a good clip.

The lead guards were now only about five hundred yards behind them and making their way onto the road.

Dee pushed Lucy along, "Come on, Lucy." His voice sounded desperate.

The feather flamed in Lucy's pocket.

Some say that if you have one of Shuka's feathers, she will come to your aid. The memory of Zi's voice floated into her consciousness.

Shuka! she thought. Lucy pulled the feather from her pocket and held it aloft. "Shuka!" she called. "Shuka, we need your aid!"

The lead archer called out, "Ready ..." The archers drew arrows from their quivers.

The air between the children and the archers shimmered.

"Lucy, run!" Dee screamed, trying to pull her along.

"Nock!" The arrows were fitted to the bowstrings.

"Dee!" Lucy dug her heels in, forcing Dee to stop. She pointed.

A ball of flame formed and hovered over the road.

"Loose!" cried the captain of the archers.

Dee flinched as an arrow whizzed by his ear.

There was a clap of thunder. Out of the flames rose Shuka, wings outstretched. She was far larger than Lucy and Dee had seen her before. She crisscrossed the road and a wall of fire spread between the bowmen and the children. The rain of arrows was incinerated in the flames.

"Stay!" called the captain. His men were already stepping back uncertainly.

The wall of fire advanced on the archers. They turned and ran as it drove them back into the forest and toward their boats.

It was the strangest fire Lucy had ever seen. It didn't harm the vegetation but destroyed any arrows hurtling toward them.

Yidi stood a short distance away, his mouth opening and closing.

"How did you do that?" he finally called out.

Lucy took one last look at the retreating flames. When they reached the water, they hovered there until the boats pushed out into the river, then they winked out.

"Zi, one of the Xami, said she might come to our aid. So I thought I'd try," Lucy said as she turned and continued limping along the road.

"She is supposed to appear to lead us back to the tunnel. I hope the fact she didn't stay with us means we are on the right path," Dee said. "Come on, we still have a long way to go."

By late afternoon they were exhausted.

"It looks like a lake over there," Dee pointed. "Let's stop there for the night. We need to rest and to find some food."

Foraging for food that evening did not start well. Yidi refused to help under any circumstances. "You will provide me with a proper meal," he demanded. "It is my right as your Exalted Ruler."

"Not my Exalted Ruler," said Lucy

"Or mine," agreed Dee. "Remember? We don't come from here. And right now, you need us more than we need you."

Yidi shot Dee a look of dislike. He found a large, flat rock and plopped himself down on it, arms firmly crossed over his chest.

Lucy motioned to Dee to follow her, and they walked down the riverbank to the edge of the water. Gull-like birds yelped and screeched above them. Lucy immediately sat down on a fallen log to rest. Her injured leg throbbed; the day's travels hadn't done it any good at all. Yidi was really getting on her nerves and his behavior raised other questions.

"Dee, I'm not sure what we're doing here anymore." She cupped her chin in her hand. "Lord Petram said our mission was to keep Yidi safe until he came of age. And he sure is in danger. More danger than you or I expected." She paused and scrabbled beside her for a moment before selecting a flat pebble to skim across the surface of the water. "Why on earth does Lord Petram want this kid on the throne? He and the Xami must think that Yidi would be a better ruler than Xixi, but he sure doesn't seem fit to rule."

"Maybe just because it is lawful and preserves order. The throne is rightfully his," Dee pointed out. "And three years is a long time. He could change a lot as he gets older."

"For the better?" Lucy wrinkled her nose.

"Look, Lucy. It's not up to us to decide who is and isn't a good ruler for this country. What do we know about it anyway?" Dee said.

She stared into a deep pool of water that had collected between two natural outcrops. She jerked back. She thought she'd seen the queen's face.

"You okay?" Dee said as a large fish rose to the surface to snap at an insect.

"Sure, just a trick of the light." Lucy knew the queen couldn't have been watching her from the pool of water. But the idea of the queen somehow spying on her gave her the creeps and reminded her just how dangerous this mission had become.

"Right now, we seem to be stuck here. Let's survive tonight and see if we can figure out where we are tomorrow. We have to get back to the Silk Road."

There was a rustle in the bushes, a flash of black and gold. It was gone as soon as Lucy noticed it, but it gave her an uneasy feeling. She wondered if Yidi had been eavesdropping. She'd meant everything she'd said, but still ... She shrugged. She'd probably just glimpsed a bird. She turned back to Dee. "Have you ever fished before?"

Dee shook his head. "You?"

Lucy shook her head and sighed. "It can't be that hard to figure out. Humans have been doing it for a million years. Do you have anything in there"—she waved a hand at his lab coat—"that resembles a hook? And we'll need some line and a branch for a rod."

Dee shrugged. "Why would I have a fishing hook? Or line? Or

anything to clean a fish with. Look, the sun is starting to set. We have to find something quickly before it's dark."

An eagle flew down and brought its feet forward as it skimmed the surface of the water. Its talons dipped below the surface, and it lifted into the air again, a large silver fish struggling in its grasp. As it rose, the bird turned the fish in its talons so the head faced forward.

"Did you see that?" Dee turned to Lucy. "It does that so it's more aerodynamic. Decreases wind resistance," he explained at her look of incomprehension.

"If only fishing was that simple," Lucy said gloomily. She'd just about given up hope of being fed that night when she realized something. She smacked her forehead. "Dee, it's so simple I feel like an idiot. What did we leave Yidi sitting on?"

Dee looked at her strangely. "A rock. Why?"

"A rock, Dee! Just like we're sitting on now. We must be stupid. We can call Lord Petram, and he'll give us a decent meal."

"Of course! Lucy, you're a star." Dee started to head back to join Yidi.

Lucy tried to stand to follow and let out a shriek as her leg buckled under her. She tried to stand again.

"Hold on just a minute." Dee returned and crouched down to look at her leg. "It's not looking good, Lucy." He shook his head at the inflamed flesh bulging over the filthy bandage. "Stay seated and I'll clean it again."

Lucy plopped down on a tussock of grass and unwrapped the makeshift bandage. Pus oozed from the wound and her stomach heaved.

Opening his lab coat, Dee took out the same bottle of antiseptic soap he had used to disinfect the bite before.

"Don't look at it if it makes you feel queasy," Dee instructed her. "And give me that bandage."

Lucy obediently turned her face away and felt Dee take the bandage from her outstretched hand. She winced as he doused the wound with the antiseptic and rebound her leg.

"Alright," he stood from his crouched position. "I'm going to wash the first bandage in the river. The water looks clean here. And then we'll have a spare." He put his first-aid materials away. "So, what are we going to do about Yidi?"

Lucy struggled to her feet. She saw Dee had torn the other sleeve from his lab coat to use as the fresh bandage. "Realistically, I'm not going to be able to leave him out in the middle of nowhere on his own. It would be wrong. His chances of surviving wouldn't be very good, and I don't think I could live with his death on my conscience." She paused to test putting some weight on her injured leg. It felt a bit better since Dee had cleaned and rebandaged it. "And if we ditch him, there go your chances of getting the key to transmutation. What do you think of the idea of taking Yidi home with us?"

"Not much," said Dee. "But I'm beginning to wonder if that's why we were chosen in the first place—because we can take him through a portal. And we don't seem to have much choice if we want to finish our mission."

CHAPTER TWENTY

Lucy and Dee returned to where they had left Yidi. He looked upset but stirred himself enough to approach them to demand what they had found for dinner. Dee bit back a retort about Yidi not finding anything himself.

Lucy ignored him and hobbled up to the rock. "Lord Petram! Are you able to help us?"

Nothing happened and Dee hoped Lucy wasn't in for a crushing disappointment. Lucy called to Lord Petram again.

"What's she doing? Has she had too much sun?" Yidi asked Dee.

"Oh, shut up, Yidi," Dee sighed.

The rock rippled and Lord Petram's craggy face appeared. "Lucy!" He smiled.

Before Lucy could answer, Lord Petram's attention shifted.

"Who's that with you?" Lord Petram said suspiciously as he swiveled his eyes to indicate Yidi who was sitting on a rock with his lower jaw slack as he stared at the Lord of the Rocks.

"That's Yidi, he's the one you wanted us to keep safe—the emperor. He rules all the lands under heaven," Lucy added to give Yidi his full due.

"How are you faring?" Lord Petram inquired.

"Not very well at the moment," Lucy admitted. "Right now, we're very hungry."

She leaned on a tree and closed her eyes briefly. "Are you able to provide us with dinner?"

"With pleasure," said Lord Petram. A rock table slid out from the boulder Yidi had been sitting on and the three kids gathered around. Moments later, a stone meal sat in front of each of them. Yidi gazed in wonder at it.

Dee stared at the rock food and then at Lord Petram. His heart sank. "We forgot, Lucy." A hot stinging sensation pressed against the backs of his eyes. His eyebrows pinched together. "We need the Xami to change the rock into real food."

Yidi took this hard. "Can't you do anything right?" He turned on Lucy. "No fish, inedible rock food ... this is the limit!"

"Shut up, Yidi," Dee said wearily. "Lucy is trying, which is more than I can say about you."

The rock under Yidi suddenly softened and flowed away, dropping Yidi to the ground. "Oof."

"You will be kind to Lucy. She and Dee are here to keep you safe," Lord Petram roared.

Dee saw Lucy was holding her feather. Her eyes were tightly shut and she wore a look of intense concentration. A warm wind arose where she sat. It rustled through the grass and raised her curls into a nimbus around her head. The air flowed over the stone food.

Dee held his breath. For a moment nothing seemed to happen and then color flooded the mineral meal and it became real. The scent of roasted meat, fresh bread, and crisp vegetables almost made him faint.

Lucy's eyes opened with a snap. "Oh my goodness." She looked at her feather and then at Dee. "It worked! That's amazing! Come on, Dee. Dig in."

Yidi was already digging in when Dee picked up his knife and fork and cut into a perfectly cooked piece of steak. He turned it over on his fork. It looked real enough. *But how did it happen, really?* He looked at Lucy again through narrowed eyes. *What's going on?*

"Dee, is something wrong?" Lucy had noticed him staring at her.

"That was just so strange," he answered. "There is a rational order to nature, and this doesn't fit."

He prodded the food a few more times. He could believe the Xami had unusual capabilities; they were extraordinary creatures. *But Lucy? Lucy's just my ordinary best friend. And so far, the feather has produced a flame like a candle—okay, that was inexplicable—but it's never transformed anything. Could it really do so now?*

He looked closely at his companions. Yidi and Lucy didn't seem to be suffering any ill effects, and he was very hungry. With a sigh, he lifted the first forkful to his lips.

Lord Petram watched them eat for a few minutes. Then his forehead creased as he asked his next question. "Why are you out in the middle of nowhere? And Lucy, you appear injured."

"Well first the Xami took us to the palace," Lucy started.

"And then we met Yidi—" Dee continued.

"Dee made this amazing silver tree. It was magic!" Lucy's eyes shone.

Yidi spoke up, "And we had to hide the silver apples from Xixi, and we overheard her talking about executing nobles and a rebellion—"

"A rebellion?" Lord Petram interrupted. "Why?"

Yidi nodded. "In Midlein province. They say the tribute is too high and they don't understand why I don't intervene. So it seems they're angry with Xixi but might not be too keen on me either." He cut up another piece of roast duck.

"And Sabu shape-shifted." Lucy speared her fork in the air as she talked over him. "And Xixi's a witch! She made a book fly through the air and she's going to do something unspeakable with two somethings."

"Sabu said the queen should send Yidi, Lucy, and me to deal with the rebels to get rid of us," Dee said. "I believe he said they would tear us to pieces," he added striving for accuracy.

"And we decided to escape before she could do that," Yidi finished. "The traitor. She will pay," he whispered as he stabbed another piece of duck.

There was a stunned silence from Lord Petram as he appeared to assimilate this information. "But you still haven't told me why you're injured, Lucy."

"Oh, a close encounter with river eels," Lucy tried to dismiss her ordeal with an airy wave.

"Oh, you poor girl." Lord Petram paused in thought before continuing. "I see. Rebels and witches and eels, oh my!"

The Lord of Rock looked grave. "It seems clear the danger we sensed was twofold. The emperor is in danger from both the queen and from rebels trying to overthrow the throne. This is serious. What is your plan?"

Dee cleared his throat, exchanging a glance with Lucy. Yidi squirmed in his seat and stared down at his food.

"Well," Dee said, "we have no idea where to take him in Sericea, so we were thinking of taking him back to our world."

Yidi's head snapped up at this, and he fixed a hard stare on Dee.

Dee hesitated a moment before continuing. "Although we have no idea how that will go over with Lucy's parents and my aunt. But it's just until he's old enough to take the throne. It's not an ideal solution." Dee tore off a bit of bread. "But what other options are there?" He popped the bread into his mouth.

"In three years, the queen might have gained even more power," Lord Petram pointed out. "He will be in danger as long as she is around. She doesn't sound like she will give up power willingly."

"Are you saying we need to defeat the queen?" Dee almost choked on his mouthful.

Lord Petram's eyebrows rose. "Let's think about it, Dee. It removes the danger to Yidi, and it might remove the threat of rebellion if he proves to be a better ruler than her."

"How can we defeat her? It's impossible," Dee spluttered. "She has powers we don't even know the extent of. That Sabu has a cunning and vicious mind. Who knows what he'll come up with next?" He shuddered. "And she has control of the military. No, we've got to head back to the entrance to the Silk Road and then straight home."

"You say impossible." Lord Petram didn't look pleased. "How do you know it is impossible until you have tried?"

"Lord Petram, with respect, sir, I've learned many things are impossible after I've tried them," Dee said firmly. "A lot of them involved explosions."

Lord Petram winced, and Dee hurried on, remembering one of those explosions had hurt the rock lord. "Some things are too risky to try to prove impossible, and taking on the queen right now is one of them," Dee said. "That result could be far worse than one of my previous explosions. Taking on the queen might have dire consequences. Lucy? Yidi? What do you think?"

"I agree," said Lucy.

"Taking on Xixi would be pure madness," Yidi concurred. "We have no armies, no powerful allies, not even a weapon between us."

"Lord Petram," Lucy started, but before she could say more, the rock lord's face seemed to ripple.

"I have to leave you," he said. "Something is very wrong elsewhere."

And he was gone.

Whew, thought Dee. *I don't know what I would have done if Lord Petram had kept pushing. No way I'm going up against the queen.*

"Blast," said Lucy. "I was going to ask him how we get back and if he'll be able to disguise the entrance to the Silk Road after we'd passed through. At least we had a decent meal."

"Yes, Lucy. How did that happen?" Yidi asked.

Lucy shrugged, palms up. "Honestly, I have no idea. I was upset about being so hungry. I was picturing Zi walking out of the trees to help us and raising the warm breeze like he did in the tunnel and in the clearing after. And then it was like the same air was all around me and over the food. It was really weird," she concluded, then shivered.

Dee shook his head. It was just one more thing for his list of the inexplicable in Sericea. No, that was the wrong way of looking at it. Science made the inexplicable understandable through the experimental method. He pulled his notebook and pencil out and looked at Lucy expectantly. "Could you do it again, do you think?"

"Not without Lord Petram making the rock food first," Lucy pointed out.

"Oh, right." Reluctantly, Dee stuffed his notebook and pencil back in his pocket. He would have to wait until another opportunity presented itself.

"We'd better try to make a small fire," Lucy said. The dusk had deepened, and the temperature had dropped. Lucy shivered. "Thank goodness Yidi made us put on these padded vests before we mounted the camels."

"Come on, Yidi, lend a hand here," Dee implored.

Yidi walked away.

With an exasperated sigh, Lucy limped into the trees in search of suitable sticks. Dee set off in a different direction on the same mission. When he returned to their small space with an armful of sticks and twigs, Dee was surprised to see that boughs and moss had been collected and fashioned into clumsy makeshift sleeping pallets. Lucy's quick shake of her head told him that it was Yidi who had done the work.

It had been nice of him to make one for each of them. *Perhaps there's hope for the kid.*

He was about to thank him when Yidi clapped his hands together.

"Well don't just stand there gawping," Yidi snapped. "Get that fire started. I'm cold."

Or maybe not. Dee saw Lucy roll her eyes as she dropped to her knees and touched Shuka's feather to the kindling.

CHAPTER TWENTY-ONE

Lucy tossed for ages on her makeshift pallet. She couldn't find a comfortable position. She finally fell asleep but woke later when her wounded leg began pulsing with agony. A soft cough made her slit her eyes open. Yidi had stealthily slipped out of his makeshift bed and slipped his satchel over his shoulder. He looked around cautiously and slid a burning branch out of the fire. Using it as a torch, he tiptoed away through the trees.

Lucy's curiosity was thoroughly aroused by now, and she quietly rose from her bed of boughs. Testing her leg and finding it sore but usable, she decided to follow Yidi to see what he was up to. She wasn't happy with Yidi, but she remembered the eels all too well, and she didn't want any actual harm to come to him.

Yidi came to a stop in front of a large flat tree stump, and Lucy edged around a bush to get as clear a view as she could while keeping out of Yidi's sight.

Yidi rummaged around in his satchel, then placed some objects on the stump. He used the flaming branch to light a small stick that soon glowed red at the tip. A moment later the scent of incense wafted toward her.

Lucy strained to see past Yidi's bulky kneeling figure to what he had placed on the stone. She grew very still as he began to speak in a low voice. "I'm trying to honor you. I really am, but nothing seems to be going right. Can you help, please? I'm so afraid."

He knelt there listening to the wind in the leaves and the faint crackles and pops of the makeshift torch. Finally, he rocked back on his heels before stumbling to his feet, wiping at his cheeks. Before he swiped them from the stump, Lucy identified the photos she had seen on his table back in his room.

He brought his parents plaques with him?

The thought of Yidi's parents brought her own to mind. They might be flaky and a bit irresponsible, but they were alive, and she knew they were very worried about her—probably.

Lucy followed Yidi as silently as possible back to the clearing and breathed a quiet sigh of relief when he didn't seem to notice her pallet was empty. She waited until he was asleep—the snoring was a clue—before creeping onto her own bed of boughs. The events of the day caught up with her and despite her tangled thoughts, she soon followed him into sleep.

A faint rustling from the branches of the tree above her jolted her wide awake. She looked up and stifled a scream. Peering down at her were half a dozen ghostly shapes, vaguely human in form, with scrawny arms and legs and enormous bellies. Their wrinkled skin cast a greenish-gray glow. Enormous purple eyes with red rims glared at Lucy and then fixed on Yidi.

"Eat, eat, hungry ..." Gasping, hissing noises came from their tiny mouths.

First one and then two more swooped down and hopped toward Yidi. "Yiiiiidddddddiiiiii," they hissed repeatedly. "Soooooo hungry!"

Lucy squeaked and lunged toward the dying fire. She pulled a small bough, one end untouched by flames, from the embers. Grasping it two-handed like a club, she advanced on the creatures. She swung and connected with one of the brutes. Sparks flared as the ghoul screamed. An unearthly cry of rage came from the monstrous beings as the fiery stick stabbed through the rest of the group, dispersing them into the night. They left a foul stench in their wake.

Both boys woke and sat up in alarm at the commotion.

"What's going on, Lucy?" said Dee.

"And what's that terrible stink?" Yidi covered his nose.

"Something awful happened," Lucy said as she flung the torch back on the fire. "These creatures came out of the trees. They were hideous. They kept calling Yidi's name. They were hungry, I think. I think ..." She stumbled over the words as the full horror of it hit her. "I think they wanted to eat him." She trembled.

Dee leaped to his feet and looked wildly about.

"They're gone." Lucy managed a shaky laugh. "I used that flaming branch. They didn't like the fire."

Yidi looked thunderstruck. He cleared his throat and muttered, "Thank you."

"I wonder what they were. More importantly, I wonder how they found us." Dee paused. He went and checked the fire. "First the archers, now these monsters. It's almost like the queen can track us."

He threw another small branch on the dying flames. It flared into a healthy blaze.

"It's funny you should say that," Lucy said. "I keep having this strange feeling I'm seeing her face in the water. It's happened twice. Once when we disembarked at the Marshes of Moreton and then again yesterday when we were at the river."

"Gods below!" Yidi said, smacking his forehead. "That's how she did it."

"What are you babbling about," Dee's voice was sharp.

"Mirror magic. The queen can use mirror magic to trace people. It's one of her witchy talents."

"I don't understand. There was no mirror, Yidi." Lucy said.

"An accomplished witch can use any reflective surface, and it doesn't have to be big," he said. "A piece of crystal, a shard of glass, a polished stone. Water is almost too easy. I should have thought. I should have warned you," he muttered. "I've seen her use an obsidian vase to track a runaway servant. That ended badly for the servant, I can tell you. *And* I've heard she uses it to call up demons."

Lucy shuddered. "I wonder if that's what those creatures were. Remember when we overheard her talking to Sabu?"

The boys nodded.

"She asked him to set up two of something. Maybe she wanted two mirrors to call up the creatures?"

"But why two and not just one?" Yidi wondered.

None of them had an answer to that.

After scanning the surroundings, Lucy did her best to find a comfortable position for her leg. She curled up into a tight ball and wished she was back at home.

CHAPTER TWENTY-TWO

"Up and at 'em," Dee prodded Yidi with his foot. "It's time we get moving and look for some signs of civilization."

A faint moan came from behind him, and Dee turned to see Lucy swaying slightly. "You okay, Lucy?"

She shook her head as he hustled over to her. She pulled up her pant leg and he crouched down to examine her injured calf. The thin red lines from the eel bite had crept further up her leg, passing her knee. The area around the puncture marks was swollen and an angry red.

"We need a doctor," Dee said. He'd give anything to have Aunt Delia here now. This was beyond his basic first-aid training. It looked like Lucy had a nasty infection, and he didn't have one fun fact that could help her.

Dee's brows dropped with concern. "This doesn't look so great. Do you think you can keep going?"

Lucy stood up a little straighter and waved a hand. "Of course. Let's get going and find the nearest village." She managed a wan smile.

He got to his feet, grimacing as he thought of her injury.

"How are we going to find our way out of here?" Yidi said.

"There's sort of a path along the lake," Dee replied. "If we follow it, we might find some kind of civilization. Don't villages usually need fresh water?"

"No idea," said Lucy. "Before this, water always came out of a tap." She chewed her lip. "I don't want to be anywhere near where there could be more river eels or spying witches."

"Then it will have to be through the trees," Dee said. "But the lake path would be easier." He had to get her help, and the quicker the better.

Lucy scowled at him as she cast a wary glance at the woods. "What about the ghost things that came at Yidi out of the trees last night?"

"They probably only come out at night, and it's broad daylight now," Dee said as he scanned the woods for a possible route.

"There is a bit of a trail there." Lucy pointed to what could have been merely a break in the trees.

Yidi looked doubtful. "If we go through the trees, how will we know we aren't just traveling in circles?"

"Dee, do you still have that ink we used to mark the way back to the Silk Road?" Lucy winced as she tried to put her weight on her injured leg. "I really don't want to walk beside the water." She tottered again.

Dee nodded, opening his lab coat and extracting the bottle. "Fortunately, the undergrowth isn't too bad," he observed as he dabbed some ink on the nearest tree.

Lucy limped heavily behind him stopping every few steps to lean on a tree and catch her breath.

Dee was on high alert. Sure, he'd told Lucy the ghost creatures only came out at night, but let's face it, he was just making that up. Every snap of a twig or clatter of a bird landing on a branch caused him to jump and look up, expecting to see the horrid monsters Lucy had described leering down on them again. The faster they got somewhere safer, the better.

He looked around, finally finding a stout stick on the ground. "Here, Lucy. Use this as a cane and see if that helps."

"It helps," Lucy said a few moments later, but after a few more steps she stumbled, throwing out her hand to break her fall. "Just help me up, Dee," she said through gritted teeth. "I'll be fine. We need to keep going."

Dee wasn't convinced she was remotely fine.

"You can stop hovering, really," Lucy said a few minutes later. "I'm sure the dizziness has passed."

The sun had passed its zenith when they finally emerged from the woods. A rice paddy rolled out before them.

"Look, over there," Dee pointed.

A small figure in the distance with a flat broad-brimmed hat and a large bag slung from the hip bent over a row of green shoots. She was dressed in an earth-colored tunic and baggy pants rolled up to her knees. The trio watched the figure repeat movements—step, lift something from the bag, stoop—until Yidi broke the silence.

"I think we can stop staring now. She's just planting rice. Let's go see if she has anything to eat."

Dee checked his automatic desire to roll his eyes when he realized he, too, was very hungry.

The path veered to their left and they were able to circle the paddy and approach the figure, a peasant girl who looked about their age.

"Hey, you," shouted Yidi.

The girl turned and, pushing her hat back over her long dark hair with a stick-thin arm, looked at them curiously. "Hello." She nodded to each of them politely. "My name is Mai, who are you?"

Yidi struck a pose—legs wide apart, his fists on his hips and his chins stuck in the air. "I am the em ..." He hesitated and frowned, his gaze darting back and forth.

Mai looked at him expectantly.

Yidi stuttered a bit and finally mumbled, "You can call me Yidi. And these barbarians are—"

"I'm Dee and this is Lucy." Dee paused, and then reached out to grab Lucy who tottered on her feet, her hands clawing at the air.

"What's wrong, Lucy?" Mai rushed forward and put her arms around Lucy just as she collapsed.

"We must help her." Mai turned to Yidi and Dee. "Quick, help me carry her to our house. Grandfather will know what to do."

They struggled to get Lucy's unconscious form to the farmhouse in the distance. Dee was dimly aware of a pig rooting under some trees and the squawking of birds in the background.

An elderly man stood in the doorway. "Who is this, Mai?" he called.

"Tourists, Grandfather. And one of them is badly hurt." She gestured to Lucy.

"Bring her in and we'll see what we can do." The old man turned and disappeared into the dim interior.

"Grandfather is a great healer," Mai said as they made their way over the threshold and into a large room.

Dee let out a sigh of relief. *What are the chances we'd stumble on a healer when Lucy needs one so desperately? About one in a million,* he figured. *Maybe Shuka had a hand, or rather a wing, in it.* "How do you do, sir? And thank you." He choked on the last sentence as a great lump filled his throat.

"You can call me Zixing," Mai's grandfather said. "And lay your friend here." He pointed to a cot in the corner of the room.

"This is Lucy," Mai said as she helped Dee remove Lucy's riding pants, leaving her in her shorts and revealing her wound. "And this is Dee and over there is Yidi."

Zixing nodded to the boys as he pulled up a stool to sit beside Lucy. "Please bring me a basin of hot water and some soap," he instructed Mai.

She bustled off and returned with a brimming basin clutched in both hands and a bar of soap tucked under one arm. She set the basin down beside her grandfather, handed him the bar of soap, and said, "I'll be right back with the towel."

Zixing thoroughly cleaned and dried his hands. Only then did he run gentle fingers around the wounds, pausing to speak. "There is a great deal of heat in the redness." His brows drew down. He felt Lucy's forehead. "And she's feverish."

Dee hovered, watching every move.

Zixing noticed Dee's anxious gaze and said, "Would you be able to help Mai bring me the supplies I need?"

Dee nodded, desperate to do something, anything to help. He'd never seen Lucy in such a bad way, even that time when she was nine and had the mumps. Or the time when she fell off the jungle gym and broke her shoulder when she was eleven.

Mai took the basin, soap, and towel that Zixing had used and led

Dee into a small kitchen. She put the used supplies in a large stone sink and rummaged around in some cupboards. "He'll need these. His medicines will be in his library. He'll get what he needs there," she told Dee as she handed him a clean basin, a sharp knife, and a pile of soft cloths.

When they returned to the larger room, Zixing had a large earthenware jar and Yidi was standing beside him. Zixing sat on the stool beside Lucy's still form and ran is fingers over the infected area again. "Ah, here they are," he muttered as his questing fingers found raised puncture marks almost hidden in the swelling.

"The knife please, Dee." Zixing slit a deep X into each puncture mark. Evil-smelling pus poured out. Yidi had to look away, but Dee crouched down beside the old man, fascinated. When the incisions ran red with blood, Zixing wiped the wound with a clean cloth and then disposed of the cloth in the basin. He opened his jar and packed the wounds with honey. "It counters the infection," he said in response to Dee's inquiring gaze.

Zixing wrapped Lucy's leg with fresh linen bandages. He stood, rubbing his knuckles into the small of his back and said, "I'll check the wound every few hours. When she wakes, we will give her a tea that will lower her fever and help her to sleep. We must watch carefully to see if the infection gets worse. We will know soon if we have won, or if the infection has."

"She could die?" Dee whispered. The yawning pit of emptiness opened inside him. He couldn't bear it if Lucy left him too.

CHAPTER TWENTY-THREE

"**H**ow is she, Zixing?" Dee turned a worried face to Mai's grandfather. Lucy had been in and out of fevered dreams through the night.

Dee and Mai had taken shifts sitting beside Lucy, who was lying on a small but clean cot. They'd soaked cloths in cool water to put on her forehead, under her arms, and on her hands and feet. The night had seemed to stretch on forever and Dee had maintained constant vigilance. As much as he was deeply concerned for her wellbeing, he was also terrified Lucy would start to ramble in her delirium and give them all away. Now his eyelids felt like sandpaper.

Zixing shook his head. "It will take a few more days ... two at least, maybe three or four ... for her to recover from the infection."

Dee felt his body lighten with relief. Lucy was going to be okay. And then the reality of the timing struck him.

"Three or four more days!" He looked aghast and glanced at Yidi, who was chewing his bottom lip. "Can we move her sooner than that?"

Zixing shook his head. "That would be most inadvisable. She's in a bad state. Don't worry Dee, you did the right things. Your—what did you call it?—oh yes, boy scout training served Lucy well, and you removed enough of the venom to save her life. But the infection is deep. I've packed the wounds with fresh honey and rewrapped them in clean linens. When she awakens, I will give her willow bark tea to drink."

Dee felt stricken.

"Don't worry," Zixing patted Dee on the shoulder. "She's young and strong. The first hours have gone well. The redness is less now, and I believe there is a very good chance that she will be fine."

"Thank you very much, sir," Dee said, looking down at his best friend. She seemed so small and vulnerable. Her face was flushed, and every so often she moaned softly.

He drew Mai and Yidi to the side. "How far are we from the Celestial City, Mai?"

She thought for a moment. "About five, maybe six days hard riding," she said.

"Is that with or without armor and weapons?" Dee asked.

Mai's forehead crinkled. "Without. The extra weight of armor and weapons would slow a horse down. Why?"

"Because we're—" Yidi started.

"Just curious," Dee interrupted. "Yidi, can I speak to you for a minute?"

Dee and Yidi walked out of the farmhouse and into the sunshine. "I don't think we should tell them everything until we know where they stand. What if we told them the whole story and they went and reported us right away? There might be a reward for information about us."

"So, we just stick to our story that we got lost searching for your missing parents and then Lucy was attacked by river eels. Right?" Yidi nodded.

"It's all true, so we're not going to get caught in a lie. And they covered the mirror."

Yidi's face twisted into a grimace. "It's a peasant superstition that a mirror will steal your soul," he'd muttered.

"Still, it's useful." Dee insisted. Zixing had looked at him rather curiously when Dee had told him this story during their night vigil, but the old man had only nodded, keeping his thoughts to himself. "We should be okay as long as they don't ask too many more questions."

"Why would they? We are just lost travelers—that bit about your parents searching for a lost city, nice touch—and I don't think they've recognized me." Yidi scowled.

Dee agreed, inwardly smiling at how put out Yidi was at not being recognized. Although they were both looking considerably better since they'd each had a bath and their clothes washed, they remained incognito. He just hoped Zixing didn't ask where they thought his parents might be.

"How many people would recognize you?" Dee raised an eyebrow. "Did you get out among the people much?" There was clearly no internet here, and Dee hadn't seen a newspaper or magazine, so the only way people would be able to identify Yidi was if they had seen him in person.

Yidi shook his head before saying slowly, "No, I wasn't allowed to go out among the people. I suppose not many would be able to identify me." His face brightened. "This will make our trip back to your world simpler."

Dee nodded. Yidi was right.

Mai was preparing the evening meal when Dee and Yidi came inside again.

She stood at a wooden table busily chopping vegetables, a cooking pot ready at her left elbow.

Dee saw this as an opportunity to ask a question he'd pushed to the back of his mind. "You called us tourists at first. Do you get many tourists here?" So far Dee hadn't seen any evidence that this area could be a popular tourist destination.

Mai shook her head. "We used to, but we haven't seen tourists for years! We wish they would come back. We were much more prosperous then. They brought money to buy our goods and they also brought us new ideas. The last ones were a bit strange though," she added reflectively, her knife poised in midair.

"Oh?" Dee interrupted as he felt his heartbeat quicken. "Do you know who they were?"

"Oh, no one interesting," Mai waved a dismissive hand and then scraped the chopped vegetables into the cooking pot. "Just a couple of grown-ups. They didn't stay long. We couldn't understand a word they said."

"Do you know where they went?" He tried to sound casual.

"Over that way, toward the setting sun." Mai waved her hand to encompass the snowcapped mountains in the distance.

Dee's heart thumped and he felt a prickle of excitement as he wondered if he'd picked up his parent's trail.

They had a simple dinner of rice, lentils, vegetables, and greens collected from the kitchen garden. Yidi looked at the food and opened his mouth to say something. He looked at Mai and closed his mouth again.

Lucy stirred and Mai left the table and picked up the pot of willow bark tea warming on the cooking surface. She poured Lucy a large cup and held it for her as Lucy, barely opening her eyes, took a few sips before turning her face away with a grimace. Mai tried to cajole her into a few more sips, but Lucy gently pushed the cup away before sinking back on her cot. Moments later, she slept deeply again.

After the dinner things had been put away, Mai brought some papers to the scrubbed wooden table while Zixing went out to check on the animals for the night. Dee sat beside Lucy's cot listening to her quiet snores.

Mai pored over her papers until Yidi asked what she was so interested in, and she explained she was planning the provisions for a deputation to the Celestial City.

"It will be a long journey for you." Yidi observed as Dee joined them.

"Yes, but petitioning is better than rebellion. Rebellions have only resulted in more bloodshed and suffering for our people in the past. But I am ready to take up arms if I must." Her normally serene face was fierce.

"One of the best generals in the Sericean army is a woman ... was," Yidi corrected himself, then paused. "Mai," Yidi finally ventured, "what do you think your emperor could do to help you? If he had any influence over the queen."

Mai stopped and looked at him. "He could make a public appearance and say that she should share grain from the vast stores that are kept at the palace—"

"There are no grain stores at the palace," Yidi objected.

"Yes, there are," Mai insisted. "They must be taking it back to the palace. He could also try to stop the greedy merchants and the queen from seizing peasants' land and belongings."

"Not just peasants," Dee muttered, remembering the chain gangs they had seen.

Yidi shot a look at Dee. "Mai," Yidi said, carefully. "Where are we? I mean, I know we're in your house, but what province are we in?"

Mai looked surprised. "We're in Midlein province, Henx region." She flushed. "Oh, I forgot. You did say you got lost."

"We certainly did," Yidi sounded grim as Mai returned her attention to her papers.

Dee turned to Yidi and whispered, "Do you think the deputation Mai is involved with is the same one Xixi was discussing with Sabu?"

Yidi scowled. "We'll have to find a way to warn her."

"But how do we do that without giving ourselves away?" Dee said.

Yidi scrunched his lips to the side and shrugged.

"We'll figure it out later." Dee picked up a piece of paper Mai had put to the side and studied the strange symbols marching in neat rows.

The door banged behind Zixing as he came back into the room. "Wind's coming up," he said as he pulled out a chair at the table and sat down.

Mai looked up. "And the hen coop is securely latched? The door blew open in the last storm."

Her grandfather frowned. "Oddly, it doesn't look like a storm. Just a high wind."

"If we are going to be here for a few more days," Dee said slowly, "do you think I could learn how to read?"

"You don't know how to read!" Mai said aghast, and then quickly clamped a hand over her mouth.

Dee shook his head.

156

"Then you must learn, we will start tomorrow," Zixing said.

The next morning, there were chores to do before Dee could have his reading lesson. Mai led them outside and around the back of the house. She wore an apron with big pockets—Dee could see scissors in one—and she held a pan full of grain in one hand. Dee had noticed the garden that had provided last night's dinner and some small structures.

"Yidi, can you help feed the chickens?" Mai said as she strode toward one of the small sheds. Dee heard the clucking of hens coming from around the back.

"What? Me?" Yidi backed up. A look of uncertainty flashed across his face.

Dee suppressed a smile.

"Yes," Mai looked puzzled. "Is there a problem?" She continued to walk around the shed until they were confronted with a small flock of chickens pecking busily at the ground searching for bugs.

"I-I—no." Yidi held out his hand for the pan. "What do I do?"

Now Mai looked astonished. "You just take a handful of millet and spray it around on the ground. Like this." She demonstrated with a fluid flick of her wrist.

The chickens came running and Yidi took a few steps back. Then the muscles of his jaw moved. "Okay, give it here." He clumsily flicked the grain and was soon surrounded by the birds.

Dee stepped forward and took a handful as well and was soon flinging grain in a wide arc.

Once the pan was empty, Mai led them toward the vegetable patch. "We will have to do this quickly. I must go into town today to pay our tribute to the emperor." She grimaced.

Dee turned to Yidi and raised an eyebrow. Yidi just shrugged.

Mai stopped in front of another small shed and pushed through the door. She returned a moment later carrying two hoes and a small basket.

"What kind of tribute do you give the emperor?" Dee asked.

"The tribute collectors take three fourths of our grain as payment for working on the land. Here, Yidi." She handed him a hoe. "You start on the melons. This is a melon plant, and this is a weed. The weeds go, the melon stays." Her eyes twinkled as she gave Yidi his instructions. His cheek pinkened.

"That sounds like a lot of tribute," Dee said slowly.

"It is. It's too much. We barely have enough to survive." Mai scowled as she gave Dee a hoe.

"You move on to the lentils over there and then work on the beans." She pointed to the tall plants supported by stakes. "I'll be over there." She waved her arm at another patch of plants.

Dee started on the row of lentils. The hoe felt solid in his hands and bit into the earth easily. Mai kept her garden tools well maintained.

"Yidi, when you're done weeding the melons, you hoe the cucumbers," Mai instructed as she cast a critical eye over his weeding. "You've missed a few." She pointed them out.

Yidi looked thunderstruck at the rapid-fire instructions from this small girl.

Once Dee and Yidi had finished their rows, they wandered over to join Mai who was snipping stems from fragrant plants.

"This is my herb garden," she explained. "We use these plants for both cooking and to make medicines."

"This looks like lavender," Dee said. "My aunt grows this. She has a big herb garden too. And I see you have sage, oregano, and thyme."

"Yes, Grandfather used oregano and thyme to treat Lucy's infection. And this coriander, just here." She pointed. "He used that with willow bark to bring down her fever. What does your aunt do with her herbs?"

Dee thought for a moment. "Like you, she uses them for cooking. But I've also seen her use them to make up tonics for colds and fevers." He frowned. He'd never thought about it before, but it seemed out of character for a modern-day physician to be making herbal potions. He mentally shrugged. Everyone deserved a hobby, he supposed.

"I have to get ready to leave now," Mai untied her apron and started back to the house. "Once this tribute is paid, we will take a deputation to the Celestial City to ask the emperor for a reduction"

They had reached the back door now and were soon back in the tidy kitchen. Mai hung her apron on a hook on the wall as Zixing came into the room.

"Ah, just in time for your first reading lesson, Dee." He motioned for the two boys to take a seat and joined them at the kitchen table. A cloth, hanging almost to the floor, had been placed over the table.

A clatter arose in the front of the house followed by someone pounding on the door.

Mai's eyes went wide as she bustled off to find out who had arrived.

Loud male voices came from the front room.

"Tax inspection," Zixing murmured.

Dee looked at Yidi. The last thing they needed was to be seen by some government officials. He just hoped Lucy was inconspicuous enough on her cot in the corner. Dee glanced down. Yidi followed his gaze and gave a slight nod before they both slid off their chairs and under the table. Both boys pulled their legs up, knees under their chins to make themselves as small and inconspicuous as possible.

Yidi was biting his lower lip.

Heavy boots clomped across the floor and three pairs of legs plus Mai's came into the kitchen. It looked like the men were pushing Mai ahead of them.

"We've come to collect the tribute in person. Just to make sure you're not holding back. We've heard complaints the tribute is too high," one of them said. "Now why would someone think that?"

"You know what happens when people complain," said a second voice. There was a thump as though a small body had hit the wall. Yidi stiffened and his hand went to where his sword would be if he'd been wearing it. Dee put out a hasty hand to restrain him, then worried the officials would spot the sword where Yidi had left it next to Lucy and ask questions that would increase their danger.

A few beads of sweat dropped onto the back of Dee's hands as he tucked his chin in, curling into a sitting ball.

"And there is talk of a deputation to the court. You wouldn't be going to complain about us, would you?"

"There is no law against petitioning the emperor," Zixing said calmly.

"Shaddup, old man," a third voice said. Boots clomped and Zixing's chair flew backward, sending him sprawling on the floor. Dee's head snapped up sharply and his heart hammered in his throat.

"Whaddaya think the emperor is going to do for the likes of you? Peasant." A glob of spit hit the floor inches from Zixing's head.

Another one chortled. "Doesn't even know the queen is regent." A boot connected with Zixing's side, and the old man moaned.

Dee flinched, fists pressed against his lips.

"Self-styled," grumbled Yidi before Dee clamped a hand over his mouth.

"We know the emperor has the rights of the crown, but she holds the real power," Mai said bravely. "And we know she wouldn't let the young emperor have a private audience with us. She would attend. But the rules say we must present the petition to him."

There was the sound of a slap, but Mai's voice continued. "And maybe, just maybe, our pleas will be enough to convince them both to be more lenient." Her voice faltered and she fell silent.

"Stupid girl, you're not worth the mud on his shoes. How do you know he doesn't agree with everything she's doing? But dream your dreams," the first man sneered.

"I will!" Mai shouted.

"Feisty little thing, isn't she?" the second voice said. "We know how to deal with that sort of attitude. Just like we'll deal with the three criminals who escaped the queen's justice."

"Know anything about that, missy?" said the first voice. "There's a large reward for information leading to their capture. Dead or alive," he added with relish. "There are notices about them everywhere."

Mai let out a squeak. Dee hoped she was shaking her head vigorously and not wondering if he, Yidi, and Lucy were the criminals. But either Mai or Zixing was sure to ask questions later. Especially since he and Yidi had hid. He'd better come up with an explanation.

"Now, missy, show us your records and where your tribute is."

Mai let out another squeak as she was hustled out of the room. As the clomping footsteps faded, Zixing eased himself back down and peered under the table.

"Stay here until I signal you," he hissed.

Yidi put his hands over his face, his fingers trembled. "I had no idea. No idea at all that people were being treated like this."

CHAPTER TWENTY-FOUR

After Zixing gave a signal that it was safe to come out, he motioned Dee and Yidi to take a seat at the table, fixing Dee with a steely gaze as Dee pulled up a chair and sat down.

"Why did you two hide?" Zixing's tone was mild but there was a tightness around his mouth.

Dee was ready for this. "We're strangers here, sir. And we knew the queen was looking for three people—we ran into a cohort of imperial archers on the way here." *Stick as close to the truth as possible*, he thought. "We're not the outlaws, I swear to that. But I could see how local government officials might suspect we were."

"You're just looking for your lost parents?" Zixing raised an eyebrow.

"Alive or dead," added Yidi the ever helpful.

Dee clenched his fists longing to sock Yidi one, but his reply was heartfelt. "Yes."

It seemed to satisfy Zixing and he just nodded.

Dee's chair scraped on the floor as he pushed back from the table, and he motioned to Yidi to follow him. They went and checked on Mai and then Lucy. Mai assured them she was fine and then went out into the fields. But Dee had seen her lips tremble, and livid bruises were forming on her arms where the government goons had pushed her around. Lucy remained asleep, so they wandered out into the yard.

Dee noticed Yidi was being unusually quiet. "You okay?"

"I've been thinking," Yidi said. "When Lucy pointed out the chain gangs, I realized that people were being treated badly. At that point, it still seemed removed from me personally." He scuffed the earth with his boot. "But when it's a defenseless girl and an elderly man who I know, somehow it's worse and more real. And urgent. Look, Dee—" He held up a hand forestalling Dee's next question. "I don't know when or how I'll be able to change things, but I swear on the Xami's antlers I'm going to give it some deep thought."

The next day, Dee started his reading lessons. Zixing began with the basic alphabet. Mai had brought out her first books of fairy stories before she went to town to buy provisions for the deputation. Bertie ambled across the pages until Dee put him back in his pocket so he could check on Lucy, who was still deeply asleep on her cot in the far corner of the room.

Yidi wandered around the room aimlessly for a while until he was told to either go outside or sit down quietly. He was disturbing the lesson.

Yidi huffed and pulled one of the maps out of his satchel. He asked to borrow a stick of charcoal and began to doodle on the back of the map.

Two hours later, Dee looked over and said, "Wow! Those Xami are amazing!" He got up to take a better look. "They look like they're coming right out of the page."

Yidi snatched the drawing away. "It's mine." But he looked down with a small smile.

Zixing pushed his chair back and stood. "Would you mind if I took a look, lad?" Yidi hesitated and then gave a tiny shake of his head as he pushed the drawing toward Zixing.

The older man stood over it for a moment and then sucked his breath in sharply. "Where did you see this?" he said sharply, pointing at another image on the page.

"That? Oh, that's the medallion Xixi the queen wears," Yidi said. He had captured the intricate design and symbols perfectly.

Zixing narrowed his eyes. "How do you know that?"

"I saw it every day!" Yidi exclaimed. His eyes widened and he looked like he wanted desperately to call the words back.

There was a long pause as Zixing studied Yidi intently. "I'm beginning to think it wasn't criminals who escaped," he said slowly. "I think it may have been the young emperor and two of his friends. Now, I can see the queen wanting information leading to your safe return, but why would she say she was looking for outlaws and wanted them dead or alive? Why would she want you dead?"

Dee hesitated, chewing his lower lip. How far could he trust Zixing? Mai's grandfather had shown them nothing but kindness, but would he believe their story? Would he use the information to collect the reward?

"It's okay, lad," Zixing said gently. "You have nothing to fear from me. Truly." He winced as he shifted on his chair and put his hand to the side where he'd taken the booted kick.

Dee shot a quick glance at Yidi, who gave a tiny nod. Taking a deep breath first, Dee spoke. "It all started when Lucy and I saw what looked like a fire. But it wasn't a fire, it was a fabulous bird—"

"And then they blew up the entrance to this tunnel leading to the Silk Road and the Lord of Rock gave them a mission. Then the Xami found them and brought them to me," Yidi interrupted.

"We found out that the Xami are omens of great change—" Dee continued before Yidi interrupted him again.

"And I figured out that meant that the Xami think I'm ready to take the throne now, not three years from now. And the queen doesn't want to give up power," Yidi said.

"So Yidi is in her way."

"I'm in her way." Yidi nodded.

"And so are Lucy and I." Dee said.

"And that's why the witch queen wants us dead or alive. But I think she'd prefer dead," concluded Yidi. He paused. "I think it would be best if we didn't tell Mai all of this."

"Oh, why?" Zixing raised an eyebrow.

"Right now, she doesn't have any idea who I really am," Yidi explained. "Which is a good thing. I don't want her to be in danger too. If Xixi's troops do come here looking for us, the fewer people who know who we really are, the better. I'm sorry you figured it out. It could go hard for you too."

Dee looked at Yidi in surprise. This was unexpectedly thoughtful behavior.

Zixing drummed his long fingers on the table as he stared into the distance. "Agreed," he finally said slowly. He paused again as Lucy stirred.

"Dee?" she called out. She rubbed her face with both hands and then looked at Dee with a clear, alert gaze.

"You're awake." Dee pushed his chair back from the table. "We were so worried about you." He crossed the room to the small cot where Lucy had been recovering. "Are you all better?"

Lucy flexed her hands and wriggled her toes, then stretched her arms and legs. "Everything seems to be working fine, and the pain in my leg is gone."

"Are you feeling better?" Yidi joined them

She nodded, sat up, and pushing back the sheet covering her, swung her legs over the edge of the cot to rest her feet on the floor. "I'll have a scar, of course, but that can't be helped." She pointed to the affected area. The skin looked pink and normal instead of an angry red.

She tried to stand up and sat right back down again.

"Not so fast." Dee pulled his chair over. "You've been sick for four days now. If you're really getting better, we can leave in the morning."

Zixing came to examine her leg. He ran gentle fingers around her injured calf. "Yes, it has healed well. She can likely travel tomorrow."

"Come and sit at the table." Dee held his arm out to Lucy to lean on. "We just told Zixing why the Xixi wants us dead or alive—"

"There are notices up," Yidi added helpfully.

"And Zixing was just about to tell us about the queen," Dee said. "Yidi drew her medallion and it caused quite a stir."

With Yidi's help, Lucy shuffled over to the table and gratefully sank into the chair Dee pulled out for her.

Zixing retook his seat and smoothed out the drawing again.

"Yidi drew that!" Dee whispered to Lucy.

She looked at it, eyes wide. "Who knew our Yidi was so artistic? But what's this about the queen's medallion? Does it mean something special?"

Zixing nodded. "It means that you are up against a formidable foe. The queen is a member of the cult of Meretsa. That symbol in the center of the medallion surrounding the tiger's eye identifies the members."

"How do you know this?" Yidi wondered, leaning back in his chair. "I've never even heard of this cult, and I saw the woman every day for the past four years."

"We studied the Meretsa when I was a monk in the Caves of Wonder." Zixing replied.

Lucy leaned forward to get a better look. "So what does this mean?"

"It means she's not just a witch, she's a sorceress. This makes her a fearsome opponent. Witches usually have one affinity: water, earth, air, fire, or mirror magic. At the most, two. A sorceress has at least three and can have all five. On the medallion, that would make a pentagram. It looks like the queen has three."

He got up and walked over to the chest on the closest wall and took several straight pins from a small bowl on the top. He pinned the drawing to the wall so they could all see it right way up.

"This symbolizes water magic." His finger touched the inverted triangle at about ten o'clock on the medallion. His finger moved up to the noon position. "This image, the six-pointed star with an eye in the middle denotes mirror magic. And this one represents air magic." He pointed to the circle with a dot in the center at about two o'clock on the medallion."

"Those are similar to the symbols the alchemists used for those elements," Dee said. "She seems to be missing a couple." He pointed to the empty lower half of the medallion.

Zixing nodded. "She's missing earth and fire, but she is powerful. Powerful indeed."

"I think her favorite must be mirror magic," Yidi mused. "She sure likes admiring herself in them."

"Did she have any other special pieces of jewelry?" Zixing inquired returning to the table.

Yidi nodded. "She wears two bracelet things made of gold."

"Could you show me?" Zixing asked.

Yidi nodded.

"Wait here." Zixing rose and opened a door Dee hadn't seen before. Through the open door he glimpsed a wall covered in cubbyholes filled with scrolls and books before Zixing shut it behind him. Moments later the old man returned with several sheets of paper and a large leather tube in his arms. He handed the paper to Yidi and placed the tube on the table.

Yidi started to sketch the gold cuffs Xixi wore.

"Are there any stones in the bracelets?" Zixing said.

Yidi frowned. "Yes, blue."

"There was a blue opal in each one," Dee confirmed.

"Those stones strengthen her power over water," Zixing said.

Yidi looked up from his drawing. "I wonder if she was responsible for the white water on the river."

Dee raised an eyebrow. "That could just as easily be explained by the shallow water—rocks were closer to the surface—and the narrowing banks forcing the water to go faster."

Yidi scrunched his lips to one side.

"She didn't know about Lord Petram," Dee mused.

"Then my suspicion is she will try to conquer him so she can begin to master the earth element too," said Zixing. "I have a scroll from the temple where I studied that will tell us about the Meretsa."

He released the stopper from one end of the leather tube and gently slid a scroll out.

"Meretsa," Zixing said as he unrolled the scroll and read, "was the first, and so far the only, sorceress to possess all five affinities. Like Xixi, no one knew where Meretsa came from. She just appeared one day with her ahtam—her spirit companion."

"Was this ahtam of hers a shape-shifter?" Yidi asked.

"I'm not certain, but I believe so," replied Zixing.

Just like Sabu, Dee thought.

"Meretsa accompanied the emperor on his conquests of other nations. When their armies knew that Meretsa led the Sericean army, they fled before her, knowing they were already doomed. But that was many centuries ago."

That evening the wind picked up again and the temperature in the house dropped.

Lucy looked up from Yidi's drawing of the medallion, which she'd been studying, and shivered. "It's cold, isn't it?"

Mai rubbed her arms as she nodded agreement. She left the table where she had been preparing a meat dish for dinner and crossed to the fireplace. Her mouth made an O of disappointment as she looked inside a carved wooden box on the mantle. Replacing the box beside two half-burnt candles, she sighed.

"What is it? What's wrong?" Zixing came into the room.

"We are out of matches. It's getting cold and I can't cook the evening meal without a fire." She carefully replaced the box on the mantle. "And it's getting dark outside. We will need to light a candle soon." Mai cast an anxious glance at her grandfather.

"I can help!" Lucy said. Dee was sure his friend had been waiting for an opportunity to repay some of Mai's and Zixing's kindness. Lucy stood and dug the feather out of her pocket. "Here, use this." She held out the glowing red and gold feather to the other girl.

"Really?" Mai took the feather and, as she knelt to touch it to the twigs and branches, the glow died. She looked up at Lucy. "Is something supposed to happen?"

"Maybe the feather only works for you, Lucy." Dee said.

Lucy frowned. "Maybe. Here, let me try."

Lucy knelt beside Mai, took the feather, and touched its now glowing tip to the twigs. With a whump the wood burst into a crackling fire. Lucy sat back on her heels as a satisfied smile spread across her face.

Mai clapped her hands and quickly lit the candles. "What is this strange magic?" she asked Lucy.

"It's a feather from Shuka," Dee piped up. "She gave it to Lucy when we arrived in Sericea."

Mai bustled around closing the shutters against the chill of the evening air and preparing the evening meal. But moments later the shutters flew back with a crash.

Lucy screamed and Dee jumped to his feet. Ghost creatures battered the windows with skeletal arms, and a great howling filled the air. These had to be the same ghosts Lucy had fought in the woods.

"Hungry, so hungry," they shrieked, their eyes wild. "Let usssss in, Yidi. Let us innnnnnnn!"

A wind sprang up in the farmhouse extinguishing the candles. Dee looked around wildly, his hair standing on end. Yidi flew backward and landed with a thump on the pallet.

Lucy gasped for breath as she put her hands over her ears. "Their voices are in my head now!" she shrieked. "Make them stop!" Her gaze darted wildly around the room.

A window shattered and ghosts streamed into the room. They enveloped Yidi, knocking him off the pallet. He landed on the floor with a thud, and tiny mouths opened wide. Needle sharp teeth readied to sink into soft human flesh.

Dee lunged forward, flailing at the creatures with both hands. Mai picked up a wrought iron poker and stabbed one in the arm.

Several ghouls turned to attack them, and Yidi was able to regain his feet. He grabbed the cast iron cooking pot Mai had left on the table. He looked for an opening where he could hit one of the specters without hitting his comrades.

Lucy grabbed a stick of kindling from the pile and thrust it into the fire. She lunged at the ghosts with the torch, and one screamed and exploded. The others drew back, watching Lucy with wary eyes. Mai ran around stamping out sparks before the house went up in flames.

"Yiiiiiiddiiii!" the ghouls moaned. "So huuuuungry!"

Dee realized he was expending a lot of energy and accomplishing nothing. He took a quick deep breath and stopped flailing. He grabbed a stick to make his own torch and thrust it among the ghosts.

Another one burst into a shower of evil-smelling sparks. The remainder fled gibbering and howling as they streamed back through the broken glass.

"What were those horrible creatures?" Mai panted, slamming the shutters closed and locking them. She burst into noisy sobs.

Yidi stepped toward Mai, but Zixing had already reached her and put a hand on her shoulder. "Hush, child. They've gone. I don't think they will be back tonight."

Mai looked around wildly and ran from the room, and a door slammed behind her.

Dee hoped she'd be okay. "We think the queen has found a way to call them up, possibly with mirror magic," he said. "But it's curious. They only cry out for Yidi, and they only appeared when Lucy was awake again."

"And Lucy was the one to see Xixi's face in the water," Dee added.

"And maybe in the willow tea," Lucy muttered, drawing circles on the floor with the toe of her boot.

"Oh, man, Lucy. Really? Dee stared at her. *Why didn't she say anything?* He sighed. *Well, it was done now.* He turned back to Zixing. "Yidi thinks that's how the queen is tracking us."

"Lucy appears to be your weak link," Zixing agreed. "But that can change."

"The weak link?" Lucy's face fell. She glanced at Dee. "I got you into this mess and it's getting worse and worse."

"Yes," Yidi agreed. "It's your fault Xixi can track us."

"Hey now." Dee raised a hand. "Enough of that, Yidi. It's hardly something Lucy is doing on purpose."

Yidi snorted.

Zixing turned to Lucy. "How did you know to use flame, child?"

"I met them the night before we came here," Lucy said. She explained the assault in the woods. "I used a burning stick to drive them away then too. Never got one to explode like that, though," she added thoughtfully.

"Flame will always serve you well." Zixing nodded.

"Do you think it's possible the queen called them up? And what were they, sir? Do you know?" Dee asked.

"It's possible. And they are called Ravenors," Zixing said. "Air magic is associated with spirits and elemental beings. And mirror magic can be used to call up demons."

"Thought so," Yidi said with satisfaction.

"What are Ravenors?" Dee asked. If these ghosts were likely to come back, he wanted to know as much about them as he could.

"Ravenors are legions of hungry ghosts, the spirits of people who committed sins out of greed when they were alive and have been condemned to suffer in hunger after death. They roam the world in search of human food and human flesh. They never get anything to eat but never give up hope." Zixing ended bitterly, "We think they exist to terrorize and torment people."

"You think?" asked Dee. "Has no one ever studied them?" Zixing looked puzzled at the question. Dee pulled his notebook out and wrote a few quick sentences before shoving it back in his pocket.

"More importantly, how did they know my name?" Yidi wondered.

"They would know your name if the queen called them up and gave them instructions." Zixing responded.

"How do we counter creatures like that?" Lucy said. "We still have to get back to the Silk Road and the tunnel."

"You have already been given some power of your own," Zixing observed.

Dee raised an eyebrow

"Shuka's feather!" Yidi exclaimed. "Lucy has been using it to light fires. Does this mean she has some fire magic?"

"We don't yet know the extent of her magic," Zixing cautioned. "But Shuka's feather—that is a powerful gift. Not only is Shuka a firebird, but feathers represent air magic as well."

"I never thought of it like that," Lucy said. "I wonder what else it can do."

"Fire magic gives you great courage and passion," Zixing said.

"She's never lacked either of those," Dee said. "But you said air magic. Maybe we've seen some of that too. Lucy did this weird thing when we were desperate for food." He told Zixing about the rock food and the warm breeze that changed it to real food.

Zixing agreed that could have been air magic. "It's odd though," he mused. "I can see that the feather is a magical device, but there seems to be something more to this." He paused for a moment before saying, "Tell me, Lucy, is your mother a witch?"

"My mother?" Lucy's eyebrows shot up.

"Yes, witchcraft is matriarchal. It passes from mother to daughter, and occasionally, son," said Zixing. He watched Lucy closely.

She snorted with laughter. "My mother," she said again. "Oh hardly." She subsided into chuckles. "If she was, our house would be the neighborhood showcase, not the town dump."

"What Lucy did was unbelievable," Dee said. "But will it be enough to counter the queen?"

Zixing said. "At this point, probably not. You are up against a fearsome foe. But it doesn't mean the queen's invincible or immortal. She is still human and will have a weakness."

"There's been no evidence of that, sir," Dee said. "So it's a good thing we're going home."

"She's already working against herself," said Zixing. "A witch or sorceress is forbidden to use their powers for personal gain. The rule is there for many good reasons, the most important is that using powers for gain rots the soul. And you can't necessarily see it, much like an apple being eaten by a worm on the inside."

"But why Lucy? Why is she the one being given these talents?" Dee asked.

"Powers, not talents," Zixing corrected him. "If her mother isn't a witch, nor are any of her close female relatives, then I'm not really sure. Do you believe in magic, Lucy?"

Lucy nodded.

"That might help, I suppose," Zixing said then thrummed his fingers against his lips, deep in thought.

Lucy shot Dee a smug smile.

Dee fell silent. After a few moments he said, "How many of these sorceresses are there?"

"The queen is the first I've heard of in my lifetime," said the old man.

"Sir Isaac Newton's third law says for every action there is an equal and opposite reaction. A balance," Dee explained. "What we need here is an opposing force of good as strong as Xixi."

Zixing nodded. "Yes, there must always be balance. The world can tilt one way or the other for short periods of time, but it must always return to balance or we will be lost."

CHAPTER TWENTY-FIVE

Despite having slept for the better part of three days while healing, Lucy slept soundly through the night and woke to Dee pulling a chair up to her cot.

"Good morning," said Dee, fishing around in one of his pockets. He pulled out a bracelet. "Zixing made you this. He has combined the powers of copper and blue topaz to strengthen your abilities with fire and air."

"It doesn't matter, does it?" asked Lucy. "We're going home. Who knows if the feather has any power there? But it was very kind of him to make it for me."

She reached for the carafe of water beside her cot, but it was just out of reach.

"And we still need to get to the Silk Road," Dee reminded her. "Who knows what's waiting for us out there."

Lucy shivered and slipped the slender band onto her wrist. She looked around. "Where's everyone else?"

Dee poured Lucy a cup of water and handed it to her. "Doing the chores. When you're up and at 'em, we will meet with them to discuss what supplies we might need for the journey to the Silk Road and the entrance to the tunnel. I'm worried about the rest of the trip now that we know what we're really up against. A sorceress!"

"I can't wait to get home." Lucy took a sip and put her cup down. "While I was sick, I dreamed I woke up in my own bed, that this was all just a strange dream. And then I woke up here again." Her eyes filled with tears. She tried to pull herself together.

A small black nose poked out of Dee's pocket.

After a deep breath, she said, "I wonder if Bertie really can call up a dragon."

Dee shook his head. "I tried that. Nothing happened and Bertie looked seriously unimpressed with me."

"What about the Xami? Did you try to call them?"

"I did and no luck, they didn't come either." Dee shook his head. "I think we're supposed to figure this one out for ourselves."

"Why can't something just be simple for once? It's been one catastrophe after another, and I am so afraid of Xixi now that I know what she really is." She looked up at Dee who was now standing and looking rather uncomfortable by the window. "How can we protect Yidi against her power?"

This mess she and Dee were in was all her fault.

What could go wrong? She thought bitterly. *Plenty as it happens. Why didn't I stop to think, just for one minute?*

She had rushed into this adventure without using even the slightest amount of common sense, and now she felt powerless to do a thing about it. Her cheeks burned with shame. She was so angry with herself. "I'm sorry, Dee. So sorry."

With a clatter of feet, the others came into the room.

"Mai and I have been talking," Yidi said. "We think we will need three camels, three bedrolls, and enough food to reach the next town on our journey."

"Camels," Lucy said faintly. "Won't that be very expensive? You know we don't have that kind of money." She didn't want to say they didn't have any money at all in front of Mai and her grandfather.

"I've had an idea about that." Yidi bustled to the table and laid his sword flat on the surface. The gems twinkled in the light. "Mai, do you have something small and sharp? But stronger than a kitchen knife."

Mai thought for a moment. "I have a chisel I use for repairs. Would that do?"

At Yidi's nod she was out of the room to get it. Moments later she returned and Yidi approached his sword with narrowed eyes. "Now, what's the best angle?" he said. He nodded to himself and, grasping the blade firmly in his left hand, tried to pry a large ruby from the hilt with the chisel.

"What are you doing?" Mai's voice rose and sharpened.

Yidi looked up in surprise. "We can sell some stones to buy what we need. Can't we?" His voice trailed off.

"I know a goldsmith in town who could give you a decent price." Zixing confirmed.

"But ... but," Mai squeaked. "Those stones aren't real, are they?" Her eyes narrowed. "Where did you get that sword?"

"I didn't steal it!" Yidi huffed. His head was down, and he struggled to get the tip of the chisel under the stone. "If that's what you're thinking." He straightened and glared at the sword. "Right. Someone is in charge here, and it's not you!" he said to the sword as he picked it up and gave it a savage thump on the tabletop. Then, chisel firmly grasped, he gouged out two large stones and slipped them into his pocket.

Leaving the mutilated sword lying forlornly on the table, Yidi turned to Mai and Zixing. "Let's go."

"Can we come too?" Lucy asked.

Zixing shook his head. "Not a good idea. Yidi can pass as an ordinary Sericean. I'm afraid you and Dee would be too conspicuous in our small town. We don't want to start any talk or speculation about escaped outlaws."

"Of course not," Lucy took a step back, feeling foolish.

The door slammed behind the trio.

"Who body-snatched our Yidi?" Lucy turned to Dee. "Don't you remember him when we were leaving the palace clutching that sword so possessively? It was all 'It's mine!'"

Dee shrugged. "He seems to be different now."

Lucy wondered why. What did she miss while she was unconscious?

⌒

There was a commotion, the honking and spitting of camels, and some shouting outside.

Dee ran to the door and Lucy followed him out into the yard. Yidi was leading a string of three camels, heavily laden with sacks and bedrolls. Lucy wondered why they would need so much. Surely those were seed grain sacks on the second camel.

"Lucy! You won't believe what we've bought," Mai ran forward and gave her a big hug. Come and see."

Yidi and Dee began unloading the camels.

Lucy smiled warmly at the other girl as Mai pulled her out into the yard. "It looks like you've had quite a shopping expedition."

Mai nodded, her eyes shining. "Grandfather got him a good price for the stones. He used the money from one to buy your camels, bedrolls, and food, and he used the rest to buy us all the seed we need, for next season's planting plus lots and lots of food! I must finish unloading." Mai ran off again.

Zixing motioned to the other three youngsters to join him inside, and they gathered around the table. He had a scroll under his arm. "Yidi says you need a map to help you find your way back." He unrolled the map on the table. He showed them where they were and the fastest route back to the entrance to the Silk Road. "If you go through the Gray Lands, it will take about four days hard riding on the camels to get there," he said.

"The Gray Lands?" Lucy said.

Zixing rerolled the map and handed it to Dee before saying, "Yes, it's a vast area of rocky plain with desert in the center. The desert is immense and frightening. Who knows exactly what goes on there? However, you will just be crossing a small section of the plain on a well-traveled caravan trail. You won't encounter the desert at all. But it can be treacherous, that's why we purchased camels, not horses. The camels travel better on such terrain."

"And if it's dry, like a desert," Dee said, "the queen will have more trouble tracking us with her mirror magic."

A few minutes later, Mai came back to the room. "We've just gone over our route with Zixing," Dee said.

"I'll help you pack provisions," Mai offered. "How much do you think you'll need?"

"Thank you! Let's pack enough for seven days," Lucy said. "Just in case." She winked at Yidi remembering what happened to their original store of food.

"Nothing's going to happen," Yidi muttered.

Mai looked from Yidi to Lucy and then back again, but no further explanation came.

"We'll leave at first light," said Dee.

Zixing nodded agreement as he looked out the window. "Best to leave as quickly as you can. The weather is about to change."

CHAPTER TWENTY-SIX

Dee shuffled his feet. He hated goodbyes. He never knew what to say and he could already feel the flush creeping up his neck.

Lucy rushed right past him to Zixing, tears welling up in her eyes. "Thank you for everything you've done for us. I owe my life to you." She hiccupped through her sobs.

Unprepared for her aggressive hug, Zixing stumbled back a few steps before catching his balance and giving her an awkward pat on the back in return. He murmured a few soothing words and Lucy's tears slowed.

Yidi stood with Mai, their heads together but Dee could still make out Yidi's urgent words. "Do not go with that deputation to the Celestial City. Make an excuse. I can't explain, but trust me that it's too dangerous. Please?"

"I-I'll see what I can do," she said softly, staring at the ground. "I don't want to let the others down, though. And if it's too dangerous, no one should go." She turned as Lucy bore down on her, arms outstretched for a huge hug. Both girls wept for a few moments.

Dee was shocked at how close Lucy had become to Mai and Zixing over the few days they'd been together, especially since she'd been out cold for most of it. It made it so much worse that she didn't expect to see the other girl again.

Once Lucy and Mai had finished, Mai turned to Dee. "I hope

you find your parents, Dee. Very soon. Will you come back to visit us some day? All of you? We will miss you!"

Dee panicked as he saw her hug coming but managed to stop himself from dodging it. After Mai released him, Dee turned to Zixing.

"I will never be able to thank you enough for everything you did for Lucy." Dee's voice caught, and a fierce flush sped across his cheeks. "And thank you again for the reading lesson. I'll keep practicing."

Finally, the goodbyes were over and Lucy, Dee, and Yidi mounted on their camels. With many a backward glance and wave, they set off for the Gray Lands.

The first two days passed quickly. Everything was dull and gloomy. The sky was covered in one solid sheet of cloud, so it resembled the inside of a pewter bowl. The scenery was monotonous. Just a vast plain with occasional large outcrops of rock forming small ridges and mesas. A steady breeze blew, lifting eddies of dust and whirling them away through the scrub brush.

Occasionally they saw a caravan in the distance. Up to a dozen camels loaded with heavy packs were roped together nose to tail and led by a single person riding the lead camel. Other men, heavily armed, rode alongside the camel train.

"What would the pack animals be carrying, Yidi?" Lucy asked pointing to the third caravan they'd seen that morning.

Yidi scrunched up his eyes as if trying to recall a long-ago lesson. "Let's see. That train is going west, so they are carrying goods from Sericea. Probably precious metals and gems, spices, paper, and rice. The queen has shut the borders to ordinary people traveling, but trade is different."

"And if they were coming from the west?" Dee said.

"What is this, quiz week?" Yidi smiled, softening the words. "Possibly weapons, carpets, leather stuff like saddles, maybe some weird animals."

"Do you want to know a fun fact about camels?" Dee didn't wait for anyone to respond before answering his own question. "They will steadily walk in an arrow-straight line, hour after hour, day after day, without deviating. That man sitting on the lead camel could go to sleep and it wouldn't affect the camels one bit."

"Interesting but possibly useless information," Yidi said.

The corners of Dee's mouth drooped.

"Now, tell me what life is like in your world." Yidi went on briskly.

They spent the time filling Yidi in on what he could expect when they got back to their hometown.

"No servants?" Yidi looked so nonplussed he was almost minused. "Who brings you food? Tidies your quarters?"

"We, or rather my aunt, cooks for the two of us," Dee said.

"And my mother does the cooking in my house. Dee and I clean our own rooms," Lucy added.

Yidi's lower jaw dropped.

And then there was the topic of school.

And where Yidi would stay. Dee offered to have Yidi stay at his house. He figured it would be less of a shock for Yidi than Lucy's rather chaotic household. And he and Aunt Delia certainly had extra bedrooms.

"Great idea, Dee," Lucy chimed in. "Our house is pretty small. And my parents are beyond embarrassing." She ended on an eyeroll.

As they talked, Dee looked around at the desolate landscape. His camel skirted some dead trees, stumbling slightly over some fallen branches.

It was quiet now. Almost too quiet. No one was pursuing them. No Ravenors swept out from behind the boulders, strewn like a giant's game of marbles, around them.

He felt uneasy.

On the third day, the sky changed. Thick black clouds rolled in, and the wind picked up.

"I think we'd better find cover for the night," Lucy said. "What do you think of looking there?" She pointed to a rocky outcrop. "There seems to be a cave of some sort."

Dee nodded. "We can check it out. It might do if it's not the home of some wild animal, like a lion or hyena. Or worse, bats."

"Afraid of bats?" Yidi raised an eyebrow, but he was asking in the spirit of inquiry, not in his previous mocking manner.

Dee shook his head. "No. But their guano can be very dangerous, and we don't need that right now."

"Dangerous, how?" asked Lucy. She'd had about enough of dangerous creatures.

"There is a fungus that grows on it that causes a terrible lung disease."

Yidi gave him a look of disbelief.

"What? I read it in one of Aunt Delia's medical journals," Dee said.

Fat drops of rain began to fall, slowly at first, but it soon seemed like a solid sheet of water had been thrown over them. They tethered the camels in the shelter of a small overhang and, grabbing their bedrolls and some food, clambered up the hill to the entrance of the cave.

"We'll smell the guano before it can actually do us any harm, won't we?" Lucy's teeth began to chatter with the soaking she was getting. "There's nothing except a musty smell. But it seems to just be a tunnel, Dee."

"We might as well explore it," Dee said. "I feel air moving through it, so there's something larger ahead."

Yidi nodded. "Wait, we forgot something," he said, throwing his bedroll into the entrance and slip sliding down the slope. He returned a few minutes later carrying some dead branches. "They're pretty dry. I noticed them when we tethered the camels." He handed one each to Lucy and Dee. "We need to light them to see and to make a fire." He picked up his bedroll again, tucking it under one arm.

They all stood in the entrance to the cave as Lucy used her feather to light their torches. They illuminated trickles of moisture on the inky walls and a tunnel at the back of the small cave. The flame cast an eerie glow in the low-ceilinged tunnel that sloped gently downward. As they crept cautiously forward, the walls dried, and the air lost its smell of wet cement. All Dee heard now were their loud breaths and the crunch of loose stones under their feet.

The tunnel seemed to go on forever.

"What if you're wrong, Dee?" Panic edged Lucy's voice.

"I think we're going to be fine." Dee tried to ignore the flicker of doubt that rose up.

Deep gouges appeared in the floor of the tunnel. The thought occurred to Dee that there still might be savage wild animals at the other end. Maybe they should have thought this through a little better.

He was just about to suggest they turn back when they rounded a bend and the tunnel opened into an enormous cavern.

CHAPTER TWENTY-SEVEN

"**O**h! Thank goodness you were right!" Lucy let out a sigh of relief as they walked to the center of a large cave and looked around.

Multifaceted gems gleamed in the ceiling and the walls.

"Look at the beautiful jewels, Dee." Lucy turned to him.

His body had stiffened. "Not jewels, Lucy. Eyes."

A plop sounded behind them followed by a second and third dull thud.

Lucy turned and froze, paralyzed with fear.

Three fat spiders the size of elephants and covered in a thick gray fur stood between the trio and the mouth of the tunnel. An eerie glow shone from each spider's three rows of eyes, all holding malevolent stares.

"Here's a fun fact about spiders," Dee said, trying to edge his way backward. He turned his ankle on a loose stone, and his voice wobbled. "Did you know that they could theoretically eat every human on earth in one year and still be hungry?"

"And this is supposed to make us feel better because . . . ?" Lucy glared at him.

Claws scraped on stone as the spiders advanced on long, spindly legs. Their fangs clicked open and shut like jackknives.

Yidi brandished his torch. The flame looked small and pathetic in the cavern, but it seemed to be enough to make the spiders stop and think. "This won't hold them off for long," he said.

Dee opened his lab coat, took out three vials and a beaker. The cap on the first bottle stuck and he struggled with it, losing valuable seconds.

"Come on, come on," Yidi muttered. "Here, give it to me." He didn't waste time trying to get the cap off, he crouched and struck the neck of the vial on the stones, snapping it in two. "Here you go."

Click, click, came from all sides now.

Dee's fingers trembled as he poured each liquid into the beaker.

"Deeeeeeeee," Lucy moaned, trying to keep her eye on all the spiders at once. Whatever he was working on, she hoped it would work.

A bottle clinked against the beaker and liquid splashed on the floor. Dee lifted an anguished face to Lucy and Yidi. "I don't know if I have enough left now."

"Keep going," Yidi urged.

Dee mixed the three liquids and stuffed a small piece of fabric into the beaker. This he lit with his torch and then he threw the beaker at the spiders.

They scuttled back in alarm.

There was a shower of sparks, a faint pop, and a thin thread of smoke. Then nothing.

"Gah!" Dee clutched his hair with both hands as he stared in disbelief. "That should have been sensational." He stomped in a tight circle getting ever closer to the wall of the cavern. "I didn't have enough alcohol left."

The spiders watched his antics, seemingly prepared to let their prey wear itself out.

"Dee." Lucy's voice quavered, but she had an idea. "Lord Petram controls all the stone in all of the tunnels and caves. Right?"

"Uh-huh." Dee's voice came out in a squeak as he slid along the wall of the cavern.

"Do you think he'd come help us if I called?"

"Nothing to lose." Dee, breathing hard, pressed closer against the rock face.

The spiders took a few steps closer.

"Lord Petram!" Lucy's voice sounded unnaturally loud to her ears. "Lord P! We really need your help!"

The spiders paused in their advance. Mandibles clicked and eyes swiveled.

The rockface shuddered and Dee leaped away. Lord Petram's craggy face, glowing eerily in the dark cavern, appeared on the wall. A thick spider web hung from his right eyebrow.

"Can you do something?" Lucy begged.

There was a faint sound like a pebble sliding down a slope, and Lord Petram whispered, "I'm sorry, Lucy. There's not much I can do."

"Argh!" Lucy wailed. "You said you would help us, Lord P. Back in the tunnel. You promised!"

"I'm under attack elsewhere right now, child."

Lucy chewed her lip. "What am I supposed to do?" she whispered, almost to herself.

"Use the wits you were given," Lord Petram suggested.

"My wits! My wits!" Lucy shrieked. "You mean I've got nothing else? What kind of quest is this? No weapons, no help, nothing but my *wits*! Can't you at least give me a hint?"

"Don't lose." The Lord of Rock faded back into the cavern wall.

Lucy stared at it in stunned silence.

"By the wings of the goddess of the night," Yidi muttered as he tugged at the ties on his bedroll.

The spiders stopped their mandible clicking and advanced again.

The wits I was given, Lucy thought, forcing herself to calm down and try to think clearly.

She edged her way back toward the wall and to the left. "Dee," she called and then stopped. "Did you hear that?" she asked, her eyebrows up in surprise. "It sounded like my voice was coming from over there."

Dee edged toward her while trying to stay facing the spiders. "It's like the rotunda of the palace."

"Can we use it to our advantage."

"Scream, Lucy. Yidi, come here and scream too."

The three screamed and screeched as the sound bounced all

around. The spiders cast their multifaceted eyes in all directions attempting to determine if other threats were in the cave.

"We can use their confusion," Lucy shouted.

She advanced on the spider before her, her torch pointed in front of her like a sword. "I just want to go home!" She jabbed at the lead spider. "And see my family." Jab! "And pet my cat!" Jab, jab.

Yidi opened his bedroll and touched his torch to the edge in several places. As it burst into flame, he swung it like a toreador's cape while he advanced on the spiders. "Come on, if you're spider enough," he screamed. Slowly he was clearing the way to the tunnel entrance.

Four more spiders plopped down around them.

"Not playing this game!" Lucy swung her torch from side to side, slowly advancing. She leaned down and picked up a softball sized rock. "I'm. Just. Going. Home!"

She wound up and let the rock fly at the nearest spider. The spider took it square between the eyes and slowly folded up.

"Girl's got an arm on her!" Dee hollered his approval.

Flame flickered and roared around her. The spiders reared back.

One spider, braver than the others, leaped at Lucy and managed to hook the back of her shirt with a claw and jerk her back. She dropped her torch.

Yidi ran forward and thrust his torch toward Lucy. As the spider drew her closer to its fangs, Lucy lunged away, her fingers scrabbling futilely for another large rock. There was a ripping noise and she fell forward. Twisting sideways she managed to grab the torch and shove it in the spider's face.

The spider's scream reverberated in the cavern and the stench of its burning flesh made them all gag.

Lucy, arms around her head, rolled away from the sight of the spider in its death throes only to come up against the legs of another spider. It lowered its head, fangs bared.

The feather flared in her pocket. As she grabbed it, a tingling started between her shoulders and ran down her arms. As it passed her elbows, it gathered strength and started to feel like thousands of ants crawling under her skin. By the time it reached her hands, she was desperate to rid herself of the sensation. She clutched her feather tightly and clapped in the spider's face in an attempt to relieve the burning itch. A percussive rush of air flung the spider back to splat against the far wall of the cave. For a moment, the only sound was the clacking of claws on rock as the remaining spiders fled into the depths of the cavern. "Wow." Lucy's voice shook as she looked down at her hands.

Dee watched the arachnids retreat into the far depths of the cavern. Then he looked at Lucy who was still shaking out her hands. "How did you do that?"

"Stop talking, we need to get out of here," Yidi roared. He stamped the flames out of his bedroll and slung it over his shoulder.

Torches held high, the three ran out of the tunnel into the cool night air.

Once they were away from the cave and all it held, and safely on the other side of the tethered camels, Lucy stopped and bent over with her hands on her knees. "I'm sorry, Dee," Lucy gasped.

"What for?" Dee said.

Lucy looked up at him from under the tangled hair flopping across her face. "I promised to save you from the spiders. Didn't do such a great job of it, did I?"

"Okay, nobody thought there'd be spiders like that!" Dee waved an arm to encompass the mouth of the cave. "But you did that strange thing, clapped and created some sort of compressed air ball ..." His voice trailed off and he ended with a shrug.

Bewildered, Lucy stared at her hands. She flexed her fingers a few times. "I have no idea how that happened. I just felt so odd—all scratchy and burning, like itching from the inside. And then— boom!"

Dee dug his notebook and pencil out of his pocket. He flipped his notebook open to a fresh page. "Science makes the inexplicable explicable," he said. "The first thing is to see if we can replicate what happened. Can you clap your hands together like that and see if you can do it again?" He cocked his head, his pencil poised. "Face away from us. You don't want to send us flying."

"I can try." Lucy was still holding the feather. Facing away from the boys as instructed, she brought her hands together in a sharp clap.

Nothing happened.

She tried again, this time with three swift claps.

Nothing happened.

"One more time, Lucy. You can do it," Dee encouraged as Yidi stood, hands on hips with a twisted smirk on his face.

Lucy nodded, took a deep breath, and clapped as hard as she could. The bushes beside the tethered camels exploded in a shower of flame.

"Argh!" Lucy and the boys ran around beating out the flames.

"We need to settle the camels," Dee shouted over the honking and squealing of their mounts. "We can't be stranded on foot way out here."

It took them ages to stamp out every spark and soothe the beasts, and they were all tired, dirty, and grumpy at the end of it.

"We can try again another day," Dee said, putting his notebook and pencil away.

"Right, it seems to have stopped raining. Let's find more wood. We have to keep a fire going. That will keep us warm until it gets light enough to ride and keep the spiders from attacking us," Yidi said. "And I have to make sure nothing's smoldering in the fried remains of my bedroll," he added. He stomped off, clearly in a foul temper.

It took some scrounging, but Lucy and Dee found enough dry wood to sustain a fire for the rest of the long night.

"We move at dawn," Dee said.

CHAPTER TWENTY-EIGHT

The first streaks of light poured over the horizon when Lucy saddled her camel. She didn't have to get Dee and Yidi up this time. When they heard her moving about, they were up and readying their own camels.

"We should be at the worm farm by noon," Dee said, consulting the map.

Yidi nodded and they mounted up and rode out.

After riding several hours, the plain melded into grasslands. They stopped to have something to eat, carefully avoiding any streams or rivulets they saw.

Soon a line of trees appeared on the horizon and then, passing through a brief patch of forest, they came upon a road.

"This is it! The Silk Road." Lucy turned, her shining eyes on her companions. She looked up at the position of the sun. "We are almost at the worm farm. We made it! We're almost home." Her voice broke with emotion.

Dee, riding in front of the other two, said, "Lucy, we have a problem."

Dee slid down from his camel and, taking the camel's reins in his hand, began to lead him. As she came around the curve in the road, Lucy saw what Dee meant.

The destruction was absolute.

Yidi and Lucy dismounted and stared around in horror.

Every glass case containing the translator worms had been

smashed and the earth spread around. They joined Dee, and the three companions and their camels carefully picked their way through the broken glass littering the roadway.

"What happened here!" Lucy was aghast. "Where do you suppose T is?"

"But what? How?" Dee stuttered. "This is awful!"

Lucy bit her lip, her gaze till searching the area for the missing word wrangler. "I hope nothing happened to him."

There was a rustling in the forest undergrowth ringing the tree farm. Several bushes swayed violently. Lucy stiffened. Wild animals? More Ravenors? Her mouth dried, and she tightened her grip on her camel's reins, prepared to turn and make a run for it.

Dee and Yidi edged closer to her as the three of them focused on the hidden creature moving closer through the bushes. Lucy took a cautious step back.

Bertie popped his head out of Dee's pocket and chittered as he took in the destruction, his head swiveling from side to side.

T staggered out of the trees and stumbled toward them. His clothes were torn and charred, and his glasses hung askew from one ear.

"T!" Lucy ran up to the word wrangler and threw her arms around him. "You're alright! But what happened here?"

T looked around with a dazed expression, then his face hardened as he pointed to a large piece of paper attached to the trees. Thick black brush strokes forming the strange characters of the Sericean language covered it and, at the bottom, the flourish of a brush stroke signature.

"Yidi, can you read this, please?" Lucy said.

He stumped over and placed his hand flat on the paper to stop it fluttering in the breeze. "Oh, wow." He muttered as he scanned the document.

"What?" Lucy hopped from one foot to the other. "Who did this? Why?"

"Xixi, of course," Yidi said as he scanned the rest of the document.

"Yidi." Lucy's voice held a warning.

Yidi quickly read the order aloud.

"'I, Xixi, Most Holy Mother and Dowager Queen of Sericea, hereby condemn this property known as the Translator Worm Farm and owned by the traitor known as T for time and all eternity. It is my most imperial command that the traitor known as T be executed on sight. Dated this the ninth day of the seventh month in the Year of the River Possum. Signed ...' and it's signed with the witch's scrawl," Yidi concluded.

"She's a monster," Dee said.

"T, you must come with us. We're going back to the Silk Road. You'll be safe where we live." Lucy urged. "I hope," she added under her breath.

T shook his head, his mouth set in a stubborn line.

"Nope," he said. "I have to find my worms. I need to make sure they are all safe. The light—the light is terrible for them ..." his voice choked as he turned and stumbled away.

Lucy followed him to beg him to reconsider.

"No, no, don't come with me." He waved her off. "This is something that I have to do alone."

Bertie gave a sad squeak and put a paw over his eyes.

T continued walking away slowly, stopping now and then to turn over a clump of earth, peering closely as he checked for worms.

"Dead, dead!" he moaned. Lucy saw him dash away a tear with the back of his hand as the full extent of the terrible destruction became clear to him. Then he disappeared into the trees again.

"Poor guy." Yidi surveyed the devastation. "Xixi will have his head on a platter if he's ever seen in these parts again."

They remounted their camels.

Dee held up a hand to stop them moving forward down the road. "We didn't expect this, and we aren't too far to the entrance of the tunnel."

"You think if Xixi made it here she's done something terrible to the tunnel?" Yidi asked as he stood in his stirrups trying to see what lay ahead.

Lucy's heart dropped. She couldn't bear it if they made it this far and didn't get home.

"It's a possibility, don't you think?" Dee said slowly.

"I think it makes sense to proceed with caution," Yidi said as he urged his camel forward.

It was late afternoon when they rounded the last curve in the road.

"Oh, no!" Lucy cried as she pulled her camel up.

An enormous pile of boulders covered the entrance to the Silk Road.

Yidi stopped his camel next to Lucy. A scowl creased his face as he dropped his hands to rest on the saddle.

Behind him, Dee twisted to look at her, his eyebrows drawn together. "A landslide?"

"What? No way," Lucy drew out the words. "How would she do that? She doesn't have earth power."

Yidi's hands shook as they clenched the reins.

Lord Petram's face appeared in the scarred cliff. A piece had broken off his nose, there was a huge hole where an eyebrow once was, and one eye had been gouged.

"Look what that woman has done!" whispered Lord Petram. *"Look what she has done!"*

The ground shifted under the their feet with the strength of Lord Petram's rumbled roar. The camels skittered backward, their eyes rolling. It was all Lucy could do to stay in the saddle and keep her camel from bolting.

"What kind of queen does this to her country?" Lord Petram's normally booming voice had weakened and now trembled with outrage.

"What happened, Lord Petram? What did she do to you?" Lucy was appalled by the damage done.

"She demanded the key to transmutation. When I wouldn't give it to her, she told her guards to use dynamite! Dynamite! The pain is excruciating!" Lord Petram spit out a few pebbles revealing a broken tooth. "The earth is our mother, she is in charge, and no one should ever do anything to hurt her." It was almost a sob. "Even now, the queen is digging into me elsewhere. Weakening me. She is tightening her grip on the throat of Sericea. She must be stopped."

"Can the damage be repaired, sir?" Dee asked as they dismounted from the camels and surveyed the wreckage.

"Not here. The destruction is absolute. Miles of the Silk Road have been destroyed. The queen has made certain that no one can enter Sericea this way." A few large rocks fell from above the tunnel. "Or leave," he added, ominously.

The bottom seemed to drop out of Lucy's world. "No! We can't stay here. So much has gone wrong. She's too powerful. How can we possibly keep Yidi safe here?" Lucy spoke rapidly, stumbling over her words, arms crossed tightly across her chest as she backed away from Lord Petram. "There has to be another portal. Tell us where there's another portal," Her voice rose to a shriek.

Lord Petram shook his head. "You must wait, child. The veils between places only thin twice per year when the sun reaches its summer zenith and again when it is at its winter nadir."

"And how long will that be?" Lucy's face reddened.

But Lord Petram wasn't listening to her. He was looking at something over her shoulder.

The sun was high in the sky now and Lucy had to shield her eyes from the brilliant glare as she turned to look back the way they had come.

Her breath caught in her throat.

A huge plume of dust was moving at speed down the road. Dust that could only be caused by the queen's troops galloping toward them.

And then Lord Petram shouted, "Run!"

CHAPTER TWENTY-NINE

About two dozen of the palace guards were mounted on camels and traveling fast. Leading the pack of guards was an enormous bronze dot. The dot grew bigger, and Lucy could now distinguish not one, but two figures—a tiger and a woman whose long blonde hair streamed behind her like the tail of a comet.

Lucy grabbed Yidi's arm. "Yidi, look."

"Xixi and Sabu." Yidi looked dismayed. "This is where we're going to die, and that woman will make it look like an accident," he said bitterly.

Lucy looked at the road ahead. *What do we do? Where can we go?* The white noise of panic flooded her. *Flee!* Was her only thought.

"We have to make a run for it." She dug her heels into her camel's sides and urged it into a swift gallop. Yidi and Dee did the same and they thundered down the road three abreast.

Yidi looked back over his shoulder and then turned back to scream into the rushing wind, "We can probably stay ahead of the guards, but Sabu is gaining on us fast."

Lucy looked back, her hair whipped across her face and made her eyes water before she could focus on the tiger. Her heart crashed in her chest as she realized how fast the great cat was moving. Xixi raised her arm, forefinger pointed to the sky and circled the air.

There was a crack of thunder.

Lucy shrieked as she looked ahead. A whirlwind had sprung up in front of them, barring the way ahead. The camels slewed and scrambled to regain their footing as they were forced to stop. Lucy held on for dear life as she saw two more whirlwinds spring into being, one to the right of them and one to the left. The wind howled. Dust filled the air blurring the outlines of their pursuers and filling eyes, noses, and ears.

"What do we do?" she shrieked over the panicked honking of the camels.

A movement in Dee's lab coat caught her eye as Bertie popped his head out and began to squeak madly.

"What's wrong with that thing?" Yidi shouted, pointing at the hedgehog poking his snout out of Dee's pocket.

"That's it! Bertie might just be able to save us," Dee said, relief flooding his features as he switched his reins to one hand, pulled the hedgehog out of his pocket, and held him aloft.

Flashes of blue-green lightning crackled through the whirlwinds. Static electricity lifted the hair on Lucy's arms and ran up to the back of her neck.

"Your hedgehog? Have you gone mad?" Yidi shouted.

"It's a dragon whisperer," Dee replied. "It's supposed to summon the most powerful dragons known to man and beast," he said as he gave the little dragon whisperer a squeeze. Nothing happened.

Xixi and Sabu were almost upon them now. Lucy could see the look of fury on the queen's face.

"Come on, Bertie," Dee implored. "Please produce a dragon!"

"Yidi, you will stop this right now!" Xixi commanded as Sabu came to a halt about two hundred yards away. "I command you and your friends to return with me to the palace."

Yidi shook his head vehemently. "It's not happening, witch!"

"You will return with me. I have ways, painful ways, to make you," Xixi warned.

Bertie's squeaking intensified and Lucy saw drops of perspiration bead Dee's forehead. "Please, Bertie!" he kept mumbling.

Lucy's heart sank. She'd known the hedgehog was a scam.

"Hard no, Xixi," Yidi yelled. "I've seen what you've been doing to Sericea, and I want no part of it. You're a traitor to your emperor, and you will pay!"

"I'm very afraid," Xixi mocked. "Little emperor, you have no idea how difficult it is to rule a vast empire. If you weren't so concerned about your rights and entitlements, you might see that!"

Yidi's knuckles whitened as he clenched the reins.

The queen crouched over the tiger's neck. "On Sabu, you may take them."

The tiger, bloodlust in its eyes, bounded forward with renewed vigor, lips drawn back in a snarl.

There was a puff of eye-stinging golden smoke and a colossal bang. The smoke cleared and a massive dragon crouched on the road in front of the trio. The whirlwinds died as Sabu skidded to a stop a short distance away.

The hot, acrid smell of a predator filled the air and the camels reared. Dee managed to hold his seat in the saddle, but Yidi took a fall and his camel careened down the road.

"I am the Dragon King of the East Sea." The dragon's voice rumbled out like an avalanche and Lucy wrinkled her nose at the sudden smell of sulfur. "Who called me here?"

Lucy saw the whites of her camel's eyes as she tried to hold on to the reins, only to have them yanked out of her hands, stripping some skin from her palms. "Ow!" The camel shied violently, and Lucy landed in a puff of dust, her camel in pursuit of Yidi's.

"We did, Lord Dragon," Dee began.

Lucy looked up into the golden eyes of the dragon with a pleading expression. "We desperately need your help."

"You're right, Gracious Lady. On my back, children," the dragon ordered.

Dee slid clumsily from his camel's back as Lucy scrambled to pull herself up and position herself between two of the back spines, each as tall as the back of a chair.

Sabu collected himself to spring. The dragon's head whipped around and flame erupted from his massive jaws. Sabu halted. The queen cursed.

"Can you give me a hand?" Yidi asked Dee.

Dee, who had settled himself behind Lucy, reached down. "Come on, come on, come on!" he shouted.

Once up, Yidi settled himself quickly. "Get us out of here," he roared. "We need to get to Mai's."

The dragon took a brief, waddling run. "Form a picture of the place in your minds," he instructed them.

Lucy remembered Zixing and Mai's house, and the fields surrounding it. She felt the great beast's shoulder muscles bunch and flex as, with a broad downward sweep of his leathery wings, the dragon lifted off just as Sabu leaped, claws extended.

The feather flared in Lucy's pocket. The same terrible itchy burning sensation she had experienced in the spider cave raced down her arms. Lucy raised her right hand, fingers splayed. Red-gold sparks flared from her fingertips. A percussive boom filled the air as pressurized air struck Sabu on his box-like snout, knocking him slightly off course. But he was so close his rank animal scent filled Lucy's nostrils.

"Ah, your little witch is showing her claws." The queen stared at Lucy in amazement before her eyes narrowed with calculation.

A tearing sound split the air and the dragon bellowed. With another determined thrust he rose far above the road and Xixi and Sabu fell away below them.

"This isn't over!" Xixi screamed. "I will hunt you down!"

The dragon banked sharply, causing Yidi to yelp and Lucy and Dee to clutch frantically at the dragon's spines. There was no controlling this dragon. It would take them where it desired.

The dragon set a new course, streaking through the sky. With each whistling wing beat, his spine arched and thrust, and Lucy shifted her seat as the dragon's back muscles rippled under her.

And then everything went black.

CHAPTER THIRTY

It was the most terrible cold that Lucy had ever felt. Her lungs felt iced and unable to draw in air and her fingers and toes cramped into claws. She thought she could hear a thin scream emanating from someone in front of her but the blood rushing into her ears soon blocked the sound. Just as she thought she was destined to die in this vast, ebony vacuum, there was a loud pop and it was warm and daylight, and the screaming continued.

It was Yidi. His hair and robe were covered in frost. Lucy looked down to discover that she was covered in frost too, and she could only assume that Dee was as well. But the sun made short work of the ice crystals, and soon there was no external sign of their recent experience.

"What happened there," Dee asked the Dragon King after he had deposited them safely on the ground at the edge of a field. "Why did it go all black?"

"I received an injury."

Lucy saw then that the Dragon King had a large set of gashes along his left shoulder where Sabu had managed to sink his claws. Black blood had dried in streaks along his side.

"Poor dragon," Lucy murmured.

"Ah well, it would have been much worse if you hadn't deflected the tiger's trajectory with that well-placed shot. Nevertheless, we had to get away quickly," the dragon continued.

"But what happened back there?" Dee wondered. "Why did

everything go black? And now—" He looked around. "Oh, we're in one of Mai's fields."

The dragon nodded. "I didn't want to land too close to the house. It terrifies the animals. As to what happened—dragons can manipulate the folds and twists of time and space to their advantage. We just went through a time fold and space valley to speed things up."

"Thank you! We're so grateful," Lucy rushed in. "That could have been a disaster." She shuddered, remembering the guards and the look of rage and hatred that had twisted Xixi's face as Sabu sprang at the dragon. The memory of the queen's last words terrified Lucy.

The Dragon King turned his head and regarded Lucy with one golden eye. "I am going to leave you here. I need time to heal and recover my strength."

There was a bang and blue-green smoke billowed from the place where the dragon had been.

When it cleared, the children found that they were alone.

Lucy stared at her companions, a huge lump filling her throat. "We didn't make it." Her voice caught on a sob. "We're right back where we started. We almost lost our lives, twice, for nothing." She thought her heart would break. "Xixi is going to hunt us down. And we know she has the power to do that." Lucy wept. "And my parents are going to be really worried by now."

Dee scuffed his boot along the ground. "It all went wrong," he agreed. "And I miss Aunt Delia." His eyes held a treacherous shine.

Yidi was staring hard at the ground like he'd never seen a field before he muttered, "You're in terrible danger because of me. If we split up, or I went back, at least you'd be safe."

No one said anything for a long moment. Finally, Lucy, wiping away the last of her tears and hiccupping slightly said, "Don't be ridiculous. Your life is worth nothing if she gets her hands on you. We're in this together, right, Dee?"

"Agreed," Dee nodded his head. Yidi looked vastly relieved. "But the fact is we need to keep going as fast and far as we can to try to outrun the queen," Dee went on.

"And we need some time to figure out when and where the next portals open," Lucy added. "The way Lord Petram described it, it seemed they opened at the summer and winter solstices. Aunt Delia told me the veil between worlds thins then. We just need to be able to stay ahead of Xixi."

Yidi nodded. "Our camels ran off, but it wouldn't take Sabu long to pick their scent and follow our trail back here. They will have to travel much slower than dragon speed, though."

There was another long silence.

Yidi coughed. "We are going to have to tell Mai something that doesn't give away that I'm the emperor—for her safety—without straying too far from the truth."

After a few moments of thought, Yidi came up with a solution and they discussed it on their way to the farmhouse.

The front door opened and Mai ran out as Lucy, Dee, and Yidi trudged toward the house.

"What happened? Why are you back?" Her questions tumbled over each other as she hustled them to the dwelling.

"We were attacked by the queen and her guards," Lucy's eyes filled with tears as she followed Mai through the front door and into the main room.

"Why?" Mai looked surprised. "You're just travelers."

"She mistook us for the outlaws she's seeking," Yidi said.

Zixing, entering from the kitchen, looked surprised to see them but he quickly recovered and motioned them to sit at the table. "What happened?" He looked at their tired and strained faces. "Mai, could you bring some tea and some fresh bread and honey?"

Mai nodded. "I'll be right back. Don't start without me!"

Lucy and Dee took their seats, and Yidi pulled a stool over from beside the fire and sat on it. Lucy put her head down on the table and rolled it back and forth. Dee patted her awkwardly on the back.

"Now what?" came her muffled voice.

"Let's hear what happened and then we can make a plan," Zixing suggested.

Mai bustled back into the room carrying a tray on which sat a teapot and five cups. She laid these out on the table and hurried back into the kitchen.

Zixing began to pour tea.

After ensuring Mai was out of hearing, Dee said, "The queen demanded that Lord Petram give her the key to transmutation, and when he wouldn't—"

"The witch destroyed the entrance," Yidi cut in. "And then she ambushed us." He shuddered. "She had her guards and Sabu." He raised a forefinger and twirled it in the air above him. "And there were whirlwinds. She was determined to take us back with her. I'm not sure why." He hesitated. "I thought for sure she wanted to be rid of us."

Zixing drummed his fingers thoughtfully on the table. "She wants the key to transmutation."

Yidi nodded. "Then she will be fabulously wealthy and far more powerful than she is now."

"It's not just money she's after, turning lead into gold is only the first step." Zixing stood up and left the room. A moment later he returned carrying a book. He sat down again, flipped through a few pages, and then turned the book so the rest could see the page. "The queen wants the key to transmutation not just to turn lead into gold, but for the ultimate goal of the alchemists—to turn mortal into immortal."

"Gods below," Yidi breathed.

"It seems to me"—Zixing picked up his teacup and blew gently on the surface—"that's why she wanted you back. It's worth it to her to keep you safe until you come of age. She has decided the only way for her to get the key now, is to wait until Dee has it. But how did you manage to escape?"

"Dee used Bertie to call up the Dragon King of the East, and Lucy did something really weird," said Yidi. "Again."

Zixing looked at Lucy, an eyebrow raised.

She looked down at the table, drawing circles on the wood, not knowing even where to start.

"When Sabu was lunging for us, the feather flared and a terrible itchy burning ran down my arms and into my hands. It's an unpleasant feeling and all I could think of was trying to get rid of it. My right hand went like this"—she demonstrated her fingers splaying—"and there were red-gold sparks. Then an air ball hit him, knocking him off course. It was like after the cave with the giant spiders." Lucy frowned.

"Giant spiders?" Mai said faintly as she returned with a platter of bread and a pot of honey. Lucy summarized what had happened and ended with, "I knew what to do, I didn't feel I had other options."

"But when you tried to repeat it, you couldn't," Dee pointed out.

"No, that went wrong. I set a bush on fire instead. The camels panicked and it could have ended very badly." Lucy grimaced. "Anyhow, after I sent an air blast at Sabu, the queen gave me a really weird look. Like she was trying to figure something out."

"She's probably trying to figure out how much power you have—and where it comes from," Zixing said. "You didn't tell her about Shuka's feather, did you?"

Lucy shook her head.

"Since you're starting to experiment, we need to get you some proper training. You need better control," said Zixing.

Lucy looked alarmed. "Who is going to train me? And where?" she looked wildly around the room.

"And we can't stay here," Dee said. "The queen thinks we're the outlaws she's seeking, and she can track us back here. We need to get as far away as possible."

And find a safe place for us to hide out and regroup, Lucy thought. *And figure out when the portals open and find a new one.*

"We must find the White Tiger of the West," Zixing said. "He could help."

"'We'?" Lucy asked.

"I'll go with you," Zixing confirmed.

"What about you, Mai?" Yidi turned to her.

She shook her head. "I must stay here. We'll all starve if I don't tend to the crops."

"You have to come with us. If Xixi finds you here and the rest of us gone, it will go hard for you." Yidi said grimly.

"But—"

"Yidi is correct, Mai. There will be no crops if you come to harm." Zixing's tone said there would be no argument.

Lucy turned to Zixing. "Tell us more about the White Tiger, please."

"The avatar of the White Tiger has air magic. As a young man, I was a monk in one of the temples in the Caves of Wonder. Even in those days, the White Tiger was trapped in the wall of the Caves. We have to find and release him." Zixing stood and dusted off his pants. "And then he will train you."

"How far away are these caves?" Dee asked.

"Many months journey," said Zixing. They are over the mountains and close to the Western Sea."

Lucy turned to Dee and Yidi, "What do you think?"

"We'd be traveling west, which is the direction we think my parents were going, and we're getting far away from here. It sounds good to me," said Dee. "As long as we don't run into the queen again, I can't think of a better option. Yidi, what do you think?"

"I agree," said Yidi with a decisive nod.

Lucy smiled as she felt the first flickers of renewed hope. Their journey into Sericea had been based on sheer impulse and her desire for adventure. And it hadn't turned out at all as she expected. Looking back, she could see how impetuous she had been and how that had led to one disaster after another. Still, despite everything, they had managed to keep Yidi safe. She was proud of that. And they might have a lead on Dee's parents.

She pushed the queen's parting threat aside. Now they had a plan and three more companions. She felt ready to deal with anything. "Onward to the Caves of Wonder."

ACKNOWLEDGEMENTS

My greatest debt is to the family and friends who have supported my writing journey. My deepest thanks go to my parents who provided me with a childhood rich in books and a resulting lifelong love of reading. Anastasia, Andrea, Anne, Ellie, and Mary—thank you for reading my earlier writing and providing thoughtful feedback.

I am especially appreciative of the team at Common Deer Press. My editor, Emily Stewart, represents what authors dream of when they are writing a book: someone who not only appreciates what is already on the page but can see the story's potential if the words were tweaked and polished just so. Thank you also to Shannon O'Toole for your fabulous cover illustrations and to David Moratto for the book's design.

Thank you to my children, Sean and Maxine. You're an endless source of inspiration! And last, but not least, I am sincerely grateful to my long-suffering husband for his constant support and encouragement during my sojourn in Sericea.